SHROUD OF SNOW

Tanya Bourton

authorHOUSE®

AuthorHouse™ UK
1663 Liberty Drive
Bloomington, IN 47403 USA
www.authorhouse.co.uk
Phone: 0800.197.4150

© 2016 Tanya Bourton. All rights reserved.

No part of this book may be reproduced, stored in a retrieval system, or transmitted by any means without the written permission of the author.

Published by AuthorHouse 07/14/2017

ISBN: 978-1-5246-6444-2 (sc)
ISBN: 978-1-5246-6445-9 (e)

Print information available on the last page.

Any people depicted in stock imagery provided by Thinkstock are models, and such images are being used for illustrative purposes only. Certain stock imagery © Thinkstock.

This book is printed on acid-free paper.

Because of the dynamic nature of the Internet, any web addresses or links contained in this book may have changed since publication and may no longer be valid. The views expressed in this work are solely those of the author and do not necessarily reflect the views of the publisher, and the publisher hereby disclaims any responsibility for them.

Other books by Tanya Bourton

Sci-Fi Trilogy:
The Plight of Nimara
Return to Nimara
A New Dawn for Nimara

Suspense Thriller:
Death on the Web

CONTENTS

Prologue ix
Chapter One 1
Chapter Two 9
Chapter Three 19
Chapter Four 28
Chapter Five 37
Chapter Six 45
Chapter Seven 55
Chapter Eight 63
Chapter Nine 75
Chapter Ten 87
Chapter Eleven 95
Chapter Twelve 107
Chapter Thirteen 118
Chapter Fourteen 130
Chapter Fifteen 137
Chapter Sixteen 145
Chapter Seventeen 156
Chapter Eighteen 165
Chapter Nineteen 174
Chapter Twenty 185
Chapter Twenty-one 195
Chapter Twenty-two 203
Epilogue 211

PROLOGUE

'Come on, hurry up!' A ten year old boy shouted aggressively as he struggled to plough through the deep snow. He stumbled and almost fell with each step. Gritting his teeth, he growled with frustration. Large, icy flakes tumbled from the sky and pelted down across his face like shards of glass. He wiped his eyes with his hand that felt numb from the freezing cold and then continued to battle on, over the blanket of snow that covered the pathway across the field. Behind him was his younger sister, Ashley, who was obviously finding it increasingly more difficult to keep up with her brother, particularly since she was only eight and a lot smaller than him. Her matted hair clung to her face; each strand was clotted together with a combination of sweat and the damp air. With each painful step that she took, her ruddy cheeks became a deeper shade of red and her breath was laboured. She was close to tears yet her eyes were wide open from panic, 'Tom, slow down. I can't...'

'Ashley, grab my hand,' said Tom's friend, Adam, who was walking alongside the girl, holding his hand out towards her. His expression was full of fear and his voice trembled uncontrollably. 'Tom,' he cried out pleadingly, 'Tom, we can't just leave Bradley out there.'

At the mention of Bradley, her little brother's name, Ashley began to whimper. Tears rolled down her cheeks and dripped off the end of her jaw.

'Just keep going, we got to get home.' Tom ignored the commotion behind him. 'Remember what I said?'

'Mum is going to kill us,' Ashley whined.

'I'm not going in with you. I'm going to go home,' mumbled Adam while holding on to Ashley's hand.

Upon hearing this, Tom suddenly stopped, spun around and rapidly moved towards Adam who instantly let go of Ashley's hand and took a step back, in a futile attempt to keep some kind of distance from his friend. Tom grabbed Adam by the collar of his jacket with his face barely an inch away from his and spat vehemently, 'Oh no you don't. You are just as responsible as us. You decided to come along today and so you are as big a part of this as me and my sister.'

'Leave Adam alone,' Ashley screamed and began to wail loudly.

'Shut up! You got to pull yourself together.' As Tom said this, he pushed Adam away, letting him fall to the ground. He faced his sister and glared at her angrily. 'So, we lost Bradley. It is not our fault that he slipped away when we were not looking.'

'But…' Ashley stopped immediately when Tom shot her a threatening stare.

'It was not our fault,' Tom hissed menacingly before turning around. Without another word, he picked up his pace and trudged on towards his destination. Deep inside, like the others, he felt extremely scared and wished that he could delay facing his parents. However, he knew that it would be wiser to let them know what happened as soon as possible.

Ashley and Adam glanced at each other quickly as they both knew that they should not have abandoned Bradley. Their duty as a sister and friend was to look after him and keep him safe. Their lives would never be the same again. This would haunt them for the rest of their lives.

CHAPTER ONE

Aiden Derham, the resident priest of the Catholic Church in Punton, made himself a mug of tea and wearily sat down on his favourite armchair to rest his aching feet. It had been such a busy week with a wedding, baptism and funeral, leaving him very little time for the comfort of allowing himself a break. Punton was a small, secluded village with merely one thousand people residing in it. Many of them were commuters who spent most of their days in one city or another, using their homes as a form of retreat. A large portion of the residents were non-Catholic and attended the Church that catered for their religious beliefs. Although, Father Aiden had only a small congregation, parish work never seemed to end. The few parishioners that he did have, always seemed to need his undivided attention for one reason or another.

Father Aiden had only become ordained as a priest a year prior to this post and was full of enthusiasm, feeling a deep sense of responsibility towards his congregation. He was a compassionate and caring man who wanted to do his best for anyone who needed him. Father Aiden found it difficult to refuse anybody his time and because he was very young, naive and lacking the necessary experience, was unable to distinguish between those who genuinely deserved his attention from the ones who could only be regarded as time wasters. This was the very reason that he was constantly overloaded with work.

Father Aiden was just about to have a few precious moments to himself, watching the local news, when there was a knock on the door. He placed his mug down on the table and was about to reluctantly get up when a newsflash appeared on the TV screen. The reporter who was standing outside the prison doors, announced, 'James Dickson, who was prosecuted thirty years ago for the murder of Bradley Davis, has been released from prison this morning.'

The camera zoomed in on a man who had a jacket over his head to conceal his face. He emerged from the front door of the building with officers on either side of him. As they helped him into the waiting black cab, there appeared an eruption of people, screaming out abuse and throwing a barrage of tomatoes and eggs. There was also a mob holding up banners and boards with horrific slogans on them. One red-faced woman pumped her fist in the air with a sign on her banner that read, 'Only the demon's death will help us heal,' whilst a short, balding man's sign read, 'Burn in hell Dickson.' There was a thick line under Dick.

Father Aiden huffed at the crowd's reaction. This happened thirty years ago and yet people felt just as strongly now as the day he was initially caught. Even though he had served his time, their rage appeared more intense. Father Aiden did not condone what the man had done by killing a little innocent boy but shivered at the violence and hatred that he was seeing from the people after all this time. James Dickson had been caught, prosecuted and condemned to imprisonment at the age of thirty five and was now sixty-five. He had missed the best part of his life. Father Aiden could not help but feel that this was punishment enough. Yet the local people would make sure that he would never be able to walk the streets and feel safe ever again. Although he was no longer a prisoner but a free man, he would never be able to exercise his right to freedom until the day he died.

Once again there was a knock on the door but this time it was much louder. The banging was made by someone who was fast becoming irritated and impatient. Sighing, Father Aiden got up and was met by a face peering in through the window. At first it made him jump and he placed his hand on his chest and closed his eyes. When he opened them again, he could see that it was Miss Colson. Her face was pressed so firmly against the window that her nose was squashed upwards giving her the likeness of a pig. As she breathed, she made a circle of fog in front of her gaping mouth. Her beady little eyes swiftly swept across the room and then settled on Father Aiden who was staring back in disbelief. The woman was incorrigible. Sighing once more, he braced himself before pointing towards the direction of the front door where he would unwillingly greet her. She always needed to see him about one thing or another and the fact that she made it her responsibility to be completely immersed in every single aspect of church life, made it difficult to get away from her. If she was not moaning about the flower arranging rota, she was advising him on how to improve his sermon. More recently, she took charge of the choir and made sure that she did the solo parts. Every Sunday, Father Aiden feared that her screeching would cause even the most devout churchgoer to leave the parish. Miss Colson was troublesome yet deep down, Father Aiden knew that she meant well.

Pausing once more, Father Aiden breathed in and muttered to himself, 'What now?' As he opened the door his face quickly changed from one of frustration to an insincere grin. Through gritted teeth he asked, 'Miss Colson, what could you possibly want from me today?'

Being thick skinned, Miss Colson barely noticed that he was being sarcastic towards her and stepped through the door. She barged passed Father Aiden (who quickly got out of her way) and advanced straight into the sitting room. Shaking his head, Father Aiden closed the door. There was never any reasoning with the woman and so it was always best to let her have her way.

'I want to make confession Father,' she informed him briskly. Her voice was high pitched and nasal, having the effect of grating on Father Aiden.

'Confession is tomorrow before morning Mass, as you well know.' Father Aiden spoke wearily but remaining calm.

'I am aware of that but I have my reasons why I want to say them now.' She pressed her lips tightly together and glared at the priest. After a slight pause, she turned her attention to the news that was still focusing around James Dickson. 'So they released the monster then? He should be left in his cell until he rots for what he did to that poor little boy.'

'Miss Colson, he has served his time. Doesn't Jesus teach us that sinners must be forgiven?' Father Aiden asked.

'Never! Not him!' the old woman shrieked back. Her nostrils flared and her beady eyes narrowed. 'That evil serpent buried the boy in a snowman and left him there. What kind of sick individual would even conjure up such an act? How could someone murder an innocent, sweet five year old boy; unless he was the devil incarnate? No, he does not deserve forgiveness.'

Father Aiden had to admit that she had a valid point but felt that it was his duty as a priest to preach the teachings of his faith. 'We all need to pray that he is truly sorry for what he has done and asked the Lord for his absolution.'

Miss Colson rolled her eyes but said nothing.

'Look, I will take your confession so let's go into the sacristy.' Father Aiden moved towards the kitchen where there was a door connected to the back of the church. It led straight to the sacristy. Miss Colson silently followed him.

Once they were settled in the two chairs that faced each other, Father Aiden was about to say the opening prayer when Miss Colson interrupted, 'The poor mother.'

'What?' Father Aiden was becoming increasingly vexed.

'Bradley's mother. When the police went to tell her the awful news, she wailed. In fact, she fell to the ground outside her front door and banged her fists repeatedly on the concrete drive. She didn't even stop when they started to bleed. I witnessed it all as I was passing by to go to the post office. They had to eventually…'

The door from the church to the sacristy opened and a man in his late thirties was standing at the threshold. He looked at Father Aiden and then towards Miss Colson but said nothing.

'I won't be too long if you wish to see me. Please, wait in the church.' Father Aiden's voice was gentle. It was obvious that the man was troubled. His face was pale and his expression was eerily blank. Instead of retreating to wait in one of the pews, he closed the door and entered the sacristy. Still silent, he walked to the other side of the room and sat on a stool in the corner. He stared intently at the carpet and tapped his foot repeatedly.

Father Aiden did not know what to do and so chose to overlook it on this occasion.

'They had to sedate her and then put her in the mental home. She is still there today.' Miss Colson tried to ignore the man but found it quite difficult because he was making her feel uneasy. She knew him quite well, therefore, noticed that his behaviour was far from normal. Nevertheless, it did not stop her from talking. 'So, you tell me if a beast like that should be allowed to walk amongst innocent people. To kill a vulnerable child in such a horrific way is not the doings of a human being but a fiend.'

Father Aiden winced at her harsh words, especially now that there was another person present in the room. 'Miss Colson, am I going to hear your confession or not?' He felt completely out of his depth. Not only did he have to badger the old woman to profess her sins but the man was making him feel extremely awkward.

By this time, the man stopped staring at the floor and tapping his foot. He removed two pencils and a sharpener from his coat pocket and began sharpening the lead on both of them. The shavings fell to the floor, close to the man's feet.

Miss Colson regarded him with caution. She shrank back in the chair and looked pleadingly at Father Aiden, whispering, 'Not with him in the room. Can't you get rid of him? That's Adam Bradshaw. He was with Bradley's brother and sister when the poor boy first went missing.'

Father Aiden was helpless. He could never have imagined having to face such an absurd situation.

Adam suddenly got up and grabbed a small table that was not far from where he had been sitting. He placed it in front of the stool and giggled.

'I don't think he is quite all there,' said Miss Colson in a quiet voice, attempting to be discreet.

Frowning, Father Aiden watched, wondering what Adam was going to do next.

Sitting back down on the stool, Adam stuck the two pencils, positioning the pointed ends upwards into his nostrils and winced as he pushed them as far as they would go.

What happened next occurred in a flash.

He threw his head back while gripping the table with his hands from both sides and then slammed his head forward onto it, forcing both pencils to go further right up his nose and into his brain. He died instantly.

As blood spurted out onto the table there was a momentary silence in the room as Father Aiden and Miss Colson were dumbfounded by what they had just seen and then both began to scream.

CHAPTER TWO

Throughout the journey, the taxi driver abstained from engaging in any kind of conversation with the man sitting in the back seat of his car. His face was firmly set and his lips were pressed tightly together. He was making his feelings of antagonism quite clear towards James Dickson who was keeping his head down in silence. The driver tried to carry out his job professionally but found it impossible to remain impartial.

Even though the whole journey by taxi was unpleasant, James was relieved that he did not have to talk. What was there to say? For the past thirty years, he was confined within prison walls where he preferred to keep to himself. The only thing that kept him going was the thought of seeing his children again and proving his innocence. Each day, James would count down the years, months and days until the time arrived when he was released. Now that he was free, he felt afraid and knew that he had to adapt to a new way of life and remain strong to get through it. This was not going to be easy as he was fully aware that everyone despised him. He already experienced the animosity of the people outside the prison gates and now the hatred of the taxi driver. James knew that this was only the beginning of having to face people's hostility and that there would be more to come in the future. Even his relatives and closest friends saw him as James Dickson, the beast who killed a child. James felt embittered by their willingness to believe that he was guilty of committing such a heinous crime. He thought they would know him better than that because he had earned their loyalty and trust. James had always been there for them whenever they needed his help or advice and gave it gladly. He never displayed any nastiness or temper to anyone let alone violence. It was simply not in his nature. Family and friends meant everything to him and he thought that they felt the same way about him. The only one who remained loyal to him was his mother, but sadly, she passed away five years ago. It pained him deeply that he had been denied the right to attend her funeral. The courts granted him permission but his family did not want him there.

The driver pulled to the side of the road and waited for his passenger to leave the car. He continued to remain silent and avoided facing James by refusing to turn around. The driver had been paid in advance so no exchanges were necessary. James simply opened the door and stepped out into the fresh air. The driver, without any hesitation, sped off, leaving him alone on the pavement, facing a house that he had not seen for thirty years. His home.

The house was still the same as when he left, except for the front door, which was now a darker shade of green. James thought back to the time when he and his wife bought the property. They had just got married and had so much to look forward to. They shared the same dreams of making this house the perfect family home, full of laughter and love. He remembered when his wife told him that she was pregnant with their first child, Emily. He believed that his life could not get any better and thanked God every day for this. Two years later came their son Jack and finally, three years after, Eloise. He felt at the time that he was truly blessed and that nothing could ever spoil his life of bliss.

On the 6th January, only three weeks after they found Bradley Davis' body, his life was suddenly turned upside down. That morning, James was taking the Christmas decorations down. His wife, Anna was tremendously superstitious and was upset that he had not done it the day before. While James was packing away the Christmas tree, Jack and Emily were sitting on the floor next to him, playing with their new toys. Anna was in the kitchen feeding Eloise. Someone started to bang on the door so aggressively that Emily and Jack dropped their toys, ran to their father and clutched him tightly. Being six years old, Emily was able to throw her arms around James' waist and Jack, who was much smaller, grabbed hold of his leg. Eloise burst out crying.

'Who in the hell is that?' Anna shouted from the kitchen. She raced into the sitting room, holding Eloise protectively to her chest. She stared, wide eyed at James, who was just as confused as she was.

'It's the police, open the door immediately!' Boomed a commanding voice.

'The police? What do they want?' Anna's voice was shaking and automatically held her baby even tighter.

Not waiting a moment longer for someone to open the door, five officers burst it open, taking it off its hinges. Splinters of wood sprayed across the corridor as they charged into the sitting room. Two of them grabbed hold of James' arms without any consideration for the two children who were still clinging onto their father.

Anna held out her hand and beckoned for the two of them to go to her. They obeyed their mother, reluctantly. As soon as the children let their father go, he was forced to the ground by the two officers who had grabbed his arms.

'You are under arrest on suspicion of murder; you do not have to say anything but it may harm your defence…' One of the officers quoted the police caution to James as he clipped the handcuffs onto his wrists.

Anna's eyes had become even wider and her face looked as if it was drained from all its blood. 'Murder?' she whispered in disbelief.

James was then heavy-handedly dragged to the police car and put into the back seat. As he was driven away, he turned his head to look through the rear window to get a glimpse of his wife on the edge of the driveway, surrounded by their children. She was crying and screaming out his name.

At first he thought that it was all a big mistake but little did he know that he was about to lose everything; his freedom, his job but worse of all, the pain of losing the love of his wife and children.

It had not taken long for his wife to file for divorce and within a month, the papers were processed. It came as no great surprise to James as Anna had refused to visit him from the moment he stepped into his cell. Clinging on to every shred of hope of keeping his world from falling apart, he tried to stall the divorce proceeding by refusing to sign the documents. He even used the fact that he was in jail as an excuse to prevent the inevitable. It did not take long for Anna to proceed with the claim of irreconcilable differences. Their marriage was over.

James felt terribly nervous walking through the gate and onto the garden path. He was wondering what kind of reception would be waiting for him. In his mind, there was still a slight glimmer of hope that he and Anna could still make a fresh start and perhaps a positive reaction from the children would surely help to achieve this. He still remembered them as they were on the day he was arrested by the police but of course, they would all be grown up now and he would be a mere stranger to them.

Anna opened the door before he could even raise his arm to knock. She stared at him for a moment before inviting him in. The expression on her face suggested that she was unsure if she was doing the right thing in letting him enter the house.

'Thank you for letting me stay for a while. I only need a bit of time to get myself sorted.' James stammered nervously. He had not seen her for so long and yet the moment she had opened the door, he felt as though he had fallen in love with her all over again. However, in truth, he had never stopped loving her. Her hair was greying and a few wrinkles surrounded her eyes but she was still as beautiful as the day he first met her. In fact, age had given her an air of confidence and a sense of strength that made her all the more desirable.

'Staying? What gave you the idea that I was going to let you stay in my house?' Anna sharply replied.

'Anna please,' James pleaded.

'I'll make you something to eat and then you can go. There is nothing more to say.' It was obvious that Anna no longer wanted him. As far as she was concerned, it was over between them and it would be pointless for him to even try and change her mind. Once she made her mind up about something, there was no going back.

James decided not to press the matter further.

He took his jacket off and walked into the sitting room. It almost looked exactly the same as the day he had been arrested and taken away by the police. The furniture was a little worn and the paint on the walls had faded. On closer inspection, he noticed that the books in the cabinet were new. They were mainly books on crime and not the romance novels that Anna had always adored reading. These books obviously belonged to someone else. There was a crystal ashtray on the table. Neither of them liked the smell of cigarettes and she refused to allow anyone to smoke in the house. This rule would surely extend to the children as well. His eyes were drawn to a pipe on the arm rest of the settee. His head began to throb and he felt a cold sweat forming on his brow. He knew that his dear beloved Anna had another man in her life. He must have been really stupid to think that she would have remained single after all this time. All his hopes and dreams were lost within one split second. James turned towards Anna and said, 'I see you got yourself a new man.'

'Yes and not so new. We got together years ago. His name is Charles Wright and he is at work. I don't want you to meet him.' Anna replied curtly.

'Why not? I'd like to meet the prat who stole my wife from me.' James could feel the rage running through his veins as he said this.

'I knew you'd get like this. I shouldn't have let you come here.' Anna folded her arms defiantly and stepped back, away from James. 'You are my ex-husband, James, and you have no right to speak to me like that. Our marriage was over thirty years ago. I had so much to deal with and Charles was there for me and the kids.' Her frustration was evident and she was close to tears.

'You had things to deal with? You weren't the one who was falsely accused of murder and spent the best part of your life in jail.' James moved closer towards Anna and was aghast to see that she winced and stepped further back.

'And you were not the one who had to console Emily and Jack as they cried every night because they didn't understand why Daddy had left them. You weren't the one who had to hold them tight, dry their tears and tell them that everything would be alright whenever they were bullied by other children and all because their dear Daddy was a murdering bastard.' As she spoke every muscle on her face was moving uncontrollably, from the sheer frustration and rage that she was feeling inside for all those years and was now able to release it in one big explosion.

James was shocked by Anna's account of how the children had suffered because of him, a murderer. There was no doubt in her mind that he had done it. He looked into her eyes and all he could see was pure hatred. The look on her face sliced his heart in two. This was the woman who had once loved him. How could such passion turn to ice? He felt as though he had been punched in the stomach with a heavy hammer. In total bewilderment, he finally managed to say in a weak voice, 'You really believe that I did it, don't you?'

Anna, without hesitation, replied, 'And so does the rest of the world, James.'

'Do the kids?' asked James, although already guessing the answer. He felt a pang in his chest when Anna simply nodded.

'At first, Emily and Jack were distraught; they missed you so much. As the years passed, they grew to accept you were never coming back. They also learned to live with the evil deed that you had committed. Luckily, Eloise was too little to know what was going on at the time. When Eloise got older, she wanted to know more about her father because she could not remember him. Emily and Jack influenced her with the way they felt about you.' Anna spoke slowly. She fought hard not to cry.

'I would like to see them,' said James, softly.

Anna chuckled nervously and replied, 'And say what?'

'I don't know, just to explain… try and form some kind of relationship with them.' James spoke in desperation.

'A relationship?' Anna shook her head and sighed deeply. 'It would be their choice; they are adults now and can make up their own minds. I wouldn't get your hopes up though.'

'I deserve to be given a chance. I am their father,' said James, raising his voice.

'You gave up the right of calling yourself a father the day they locked you up.' Anna shot back.

'And whose fault was that? You didn't allow them to visit me. You certainly led them to believe that I was a murderer and there was nothing that I could do about it.' James replied with resentment.

'And would it have been appropriate to show them where their beloved daddy had gone? Take them to a prison? I was protecting them.' Anna shouted.

'But to stop them when they got older as well? How did you manage that one?' James cried.

'They no longer wanted to see you. They had Charles.' Anna replied.

'And dear Charles slipped into my role as a father and into my bed with my wife.' James spoke with vehemence and a look of disgust at the mere thought of it on his face.

'Don't you dare,' spat Anna. 'Charles had been more than a father than you could have ever been. He paid for their education, school trips, clothes, everything. He put food on our table…'

'So, it was all about money? What does that make you then?' James barked. He immediately regretted what he had just said and quickly apologised.

'Too late for that, you meant it.' Anna was shaking with rage but managed to keep a dignified stance. 'For God's sake James, we divorced thirty years ago. Isn't it about time you let go? Grow up! I moved on, so why can't you?'

'It's so easy for you to say that. You saw our children growing up, while I missed all that. It didn't take you long to start a new life with another man. I lost everything that was dear to me. If I can't have you, I must at least try to win my children back and believe me, I will fight hard to do so. You will not stop me because I won't let you.'

Anna shook her head and muttered, 'This isn't getting us anywhere.' She started to make her way to the kitchen. 'I'll make you something to eat.'

'No, don't bother, I'm going now, I need to find a place to stay. I will be in touch once I've sorted things out. Please, I'm begging you, ask them to meet me. At least for an hour or so. You owe me at least that much.' James stood up and grabbed his jacket.

'Why don't you ask them yourself?' Anna whispered.

'It will sound better coming from you.' James bowed his head sadly. After a few moments, he looked at Anna, 'I am going to prove my innocence. I don't know how or how long it will take but I will get justice.' He gave a pathetic smile and reached his hand out to touch her but thought better of it and put it down by his side. Then, he made his way to the front door. He stopped and turned once more to face Anna, 'I would have been the best father in the world to our children. I still would now, given the opportunity.'

Anna remained still without saying a word. Slowly, James made his way out of the door, disappearing from her sight as he walked through the corridor.

Anna remained where she was until hearing the front door close.

CHAPTER THREE

The coach was moving along the motorway with most of its passengers fast asleep. It was morning and the sun had risen over the horizon. Two hours had passed since Ashley stepped off the twenty-one hour flight from Melbourne, so it was natural that she was now feeling quite jet lagged. Even though, Ashley was utterly exhausted, she still found it impossible to fall asleep. She could never relax and enjoy any kind of journey. It was at those times that she felt envious of the people around her who could simply close their eyes and drift off into the land of dreams while she had to sit quietly and endure a long, tedious and arduous trek. Not knowing what to do with herself, she began to look around at the other people on the coach. There were couples that snuggled up into each other with their coats serving as blankets. Someone at the back was snoring softly and the sound somehow worked in harmony with the rhythm of the engine that purred continuously, making an eerie bass beat. Surprisingly, Ashley did not find the noise annoying but rather soothing. She spotted a young girl in her early twenties who was on the same flight as she was, hunched in the foetal position, facing the window with her thumb in her mouth. In slumber, the girl looked so vulnerable and innocent and yet when awake on the plane, she was loud and rather crude. Throughout most of the flight, she did nothing but cuss and complain. Her seat was uncomfortable; the queue to the toilet was too long; the food was cold and inedible; the service was too slow. The hostesses did their best to please her but to no avail. The passengers became agitated with her constant moaning and an elderly lady sitting in front of her, tut-tutted in disgust. Now, that the girl was sleeping, she looked angelic. If Ashley had not witnessed the girl's behaviour on the plane, she would never have guessed how horrid and spiteful she could really be. People were not always what they seemed to be. That was something she had learned from a very early age.

Once she finished observing the passengers on the coach, she needed to find something else to occupy herself with in order to escape from the monotony of travelling. Ashley remembered that there was a crossword book in her bag and after shuffling around inside, she pulled it out. Realising that she lost her pen, she put it back and placed her bag on the floor by her feet. She turned towards the window and looked at the fields and trees as the coach sped past. Here and there were houses and telegraph poles but otherwise the scenery was remarkably barren and uninteresting. Looking down onto the road, she could see the cars pass by in the next lane.

Her mind started to drift towards the people inside the cars, overtaking in the fast lane. Some of them travelling alone and others with passengers and she began to wonder where they could be going to so early in the morning.

Were they returning from a well-deserved holiday? Perhaps some of them were going to work. Others may be heading towards a celebration, a wedding, birth of a child or visiting loved ones that they had not seen for some time. She hoped that each of them would be heading towards a more pleasant destination, unlike hers.

Since that day, when the three of them returned to the house to explain to their mother that Bradley was missing, the unity of the family was broken. She could barely look her brother Tom in the face and was sickened to be anywhere near him. Tom seemed to be unmoved by the horrifying incident and was quite happy to keep out of her way and get on with his life as if nothing happened. She had once idolised her brother and wanted to be just like him but from that day, she could only feel revulsion towards him.

When Bradley's body was found, Ashley's mother underwent a complete mental breakdown and ended up in a psychiatric hospital. Even though she received the necessary treatment and care, her condition did not improve. Ashley was only a little girl at the time and was not equipped to undergo such traumatic and emotional experiences. Guilt weighed heavily on her little heart, knowing that she had partly contributed to her mother's illness. At first, the doctors were optimistic that their patient would get better and carried on reviewing her progress for weeks, months and then years. The only hope left for Ashley's father, Michael, was to place his wife into an independent hospital called Westcourt House in London. They had specialists who successfully dealt with mental health cases but it soon became evident that she had no will to get better. The doctors had explored and carried out every possible avenue of finding a treatment that she would respond to. Eventually, they realised that there was no likelihood that she would ever improve under the circumstances but remain sectioned until the day she died from a broken heart that could never be medically mended.

Ashley felt that she had not only lost her mother but her father too. It was a very difficult time for a little girl to go through and she longed for him to put his arms around her and tell her that everything was going to be alright. Ashley needed his love, support and undivided attention but that was not what she got. He not only mourned for the loss of his son but his beloved and vibrant wife, Alice. He became increasingly withdrawn and barely spoke a word to anyone. Ashley and Tom were still his responsibility and the very reason that should have given him the determination and strength to carry on. Instead, he walked around the house with a haunted expression and soon gave up his job, not that he needed to work. Not only was he prudent and managed to save a good amount of money over the years but he was left a large estate and money by his aunt in her will. His aunt had never married and had no children and no other family to leave her fortune too, therefore, Michael became the sole beneficiary in her will when she died. This left the family in a very comfortable position.

Then her thoughts turned to Adam, dear, sweet Adam, the boy who was protective towards her and a loyal friend of Tom's. She loved him from childhood and believed that one day they would get married. This was a secret that she kept to herself and one that was doomed from the start. Since that dreadful day, he refused to associate with Tom and inevitably had no choice but to exclude Ashley from his life too.

Ashley's life changed after her little brother was murdered and it would never be the same again. The close family unity and the warmth that radiated from it was lost forever. The atmosphere was gloomy, tense and soul destroying. People stared pitifully at her in the streets. As Ashley got older, she realised that nothing would ever change. It became clear that her mother would never recover and she was the only hope of bringing the family together again. From a young age, Ashley decided that one day, she would escape the hell that she was living in and try to build a new life as far away as possible. She worked hard to get a good education as she felt this would help her towards a better life. University was the starting point for Ashley in getting some pleasure back into her life. She made some good friends and was able to remain at the campus without the need of going back home during the holidays. This was also the first step towards her sole independence and confirmed that moving away to another country would be the right thing to do. After University, she carried on to take a P.G.C.E course and successfully passed as a Teacher of English. Ashley was now twenty-two years old and ready to complete her plan to move from England altogether. She found an opening in the job section of a newspaper, advertising for Teachers in Australia. With barely a second thought, she applied and once she received notification that her application was successful, packed her bags and excitedly stepped onto the aeroplane. As she ascended the stairs of the plane, she felt the weight of the world lift from her troubled shoulders. This was her golden opportunity of beginning a new life, leaving the past behind and using her bad and woeful experiences to her advantage.

Her new life was more than she could have ever dreamed of. She delighted in the friendliness of the local people and found herself feeling at ease with them. She was surrounded by a group of friends and never felt alone. If she was not working hard in the classroom, she was gossiping in the staffroom. Each evening, they all went out together as there was always something to do. She attended barbeques at sunset, birthday parties, even social events created just because they could. She had settled in so well that it became easy to put the past behind her. In Australia, she was a different person and she loved what she had become.

Try as one may to blank out all the tragedies and ghosts from one's life, eventually something will happen unexpectedly to bring them all back. This is exactly what happened to Ashley on a Monday morning in the staffroom during break time. One of the English teachers, Maddie, was fascinated by the grammar and individual words used by British people and subscribed to a magazine site that sent the top newspapers to her. It cost her a lot of money each month but she felt it was worth it.

'Ashley?' Maddie spoke questioningly as she peered at her from over the newspaper that she was reading. Only her nose and eyes were visible from behind the paper.

'Hmm?' Ashley replied while biting into an apple.

'Didn't you come from a place called Punton?' asked Maddie, thoughtfully.

'Yeah, why?' Ashley asked, frowning.

'A man, not much older than you has committed suicide. Sounds disturbing. Says, he stuck two pencils up his nose and smashed his head down on a table. Gruesome.' Maddie screwed her face in revulsion as she spoke.

'What was his name?' Ashley asked out of curiosity.

'Adam Bradshaw,' Maddie replied, shrugging her shoulders. 'His funeral is next week. Guess you knew him.'

Ashley immediately threw her apple on the table and snatched the newspaper from Maddie. She looked at the page with the tragic news printed on it, together with a picture of Adam. It looked like a passport photograph and in it, he looked drawn and miserable. Of course, he had matured a lot since she had last saw him but those kind, striking eyes remained the same. 'Yes. Yes, I did, very well.' Ashley had grown pale and her hands began to shake. She could barely hold the paper. 'I have to go back.'

The news that Adam was dead reopened Ashley's old wounds. After all those years of trying to erase him from her mind, she realised how futile it had been because his death affected her deeply. She would have to go back home to England and face all the problems that she left behind. This would prove awkward because she broke all contact with her family. Of course, they had her mobile number in case of an emergency but they had never made the effort to contact her. However, what she feared the most was having to face Tom. He would obviously be at the funeral and they would be forced to talk about things that she thought, by running away, would have been laid to rest.

Now, that she was in the coach, heading back home, reflecting on the past and thinking about the present, caused Ashley's eyes to well up, forcing the tears to come tumbling down her cheeks. She was hurt to think that no-one back home thought to ring her and tell her what had happened to Adam. She knew that it was partly her own fault for distancing herself away from the family but hearing about the news from them first, would have been important to her. They knew her mobile number, so there was no excuse.

When she initially left home, she expected her father to be concerned enough about her to at least want to know how she was getting on and if she was okay. Perhaps, occasionally, say hello but he never did. It became obvious to her, as the years passed by, that to him, she was as good as dead.

However, what concerned her the most was that after hearing about Adam's suicide, she made several attempts to contact her father but he never answered her calls. She left messages on the answering machine but he failed to call her back. It made Ashley wonder, if on her return, he would refuse to acknowledge her. Was he really so bitter about her moving away?

All these thoughts going round in her head provoked Ashley into making one more attempt to ring her father but to her horror, it was Tom who answered. Hearing his voice after so many years filled her with dread.

'Hello?' His voice was deep and husky but there was no doubt in her mind who it was.

After a short pause, Ashley replied, 'Tom? It's Ashley.'

'I take it you heard,' was all he said.

'I am surprised that no-one bothered to tell me. Adam was our friend.' She felt herself welling up with grief.

'Adam?' Tom questioned, sounding puzzled. 'Oh, of course, are you coming back for the funeral?'

'Yes, of course I am,' raising her voice. 'Where's Dad? I want to speak to him.'

'Dad? He is busy at the moment. When are you coming so that I can make arrangements to pick you up?' His offer took her by complete surprise. They did not exactly part on good terms and neither of them made any attempt in keeping contact with one another. Tom sounded so matter of fact as if everything was fine between them. His whole attitude seemed odd somehow.

'I'm on the coach making my way home from the airport. Just let Dad know that I should arrive at the house about midday because I have to change coaches midway.' After saying this, Ashley switched off her phone and placed it back into her handbag.

Now that Ashley had the time to reflect on the conversation that she had with Tom, she began to worry. Why wouldn't her father come to the phone? Surely he would not be busy at this time of the morning. What is really going on? Was there anything that she should know? Ashley knew that very soon all her questions would be answered. She was aware that a lot of things must have changed since she left but had a bad feeling that they would be for the worse.

CHAPTER FOUR

'Thanks for doing this for me, Stace, you are an angel.' Tom grabbed his jacket and kissed his wife gently on the cheek.

It was Thursday morning and Tom was about to drive to central London to attend one of his monthly meetings. He had to get up early to make sure that he arrived on time at his destination. He hated travelling to the city because once he reached close to London, he would always find himself stuck in a traffic jam.

When he first began his job as a Project Manager in Bromley, he thought he had hit the jackpot. With a salary of fifty five thousand pounds a year, plus benefits and bonuses, he could not believe his luck. However, after working for the company for ten years, it began to lose its clients who got a better deal elsewhere. They were failing to compete with other larger companies who could afford to offer their services for less money. After giving their long and loyal service, many of his friends and colleagues were made redundant. Tom should have felt fortunate that he still held on to his job but then the bonuses disappeared and so did many of the other perks he was receiving. Eventually, he was called into the boss' office to be told that he had to take a ten percent cut in his wages. There was no discussion or apology. It was taken for granted that he would gladly accept the cut from his salary and show his gratitude towards the company for allowing him to stay. The whole affair was handled clinically and coldly, without any consideration towards his feelings and financial position. He had to listen to the glassy eyed, bald man sitting behind the huge oak desk who smirked smugly whilst giving Tom the bad news. With every second, he felt his collar tighten and the beads of sweat welling up at the back of his neck. It made Tom shiver as the sweat became droplets that started to drip down his back.

His boss then laced his hands together and leaning forward explained that the company still expected him to carry on doing the same amount of work, if not more. Tom would have to work a lot harder in order to pick up more projects than ever before.

'In short, either accept it or find another job,' said the boss with a grin on his face, showing that he was enjoying giving Tom the bad news.

It did not take long after this, that Tom began to grow more tired and depressed due to the pressure of working harder than ever, tightening the purse strings to keep up with the payments of his monthly bills and spending less time with his wife because of the extra hours demanded of him from the increasing workload. Worse still, there was a threat that his office in Bromley would be closed and he would have to commute to the city every day. This would be almost impossible to sustain because of the extra distance and time that he would have to travel. If Tom found himself in that position, there would be two options left for him to consider. The first would be to take redundancy in the hope of finding another job quickly with the same calibre and wages as his present one. The second, to move closer to London using the relocation expenses on offer. Even though Tom did not like his boss, he loved his job and it was the one thing that he really excelled at.

'Tom you're late, again. Get going. All will be okay here, I promise.' Stacey smiled sweetly and handed him a Tupperware box full of tasty treats.

Tom gazed down at his wife and stroked her hair. She was the most precious thing to him in the entire world. He knew her from childhood because she was his sister's best friend at school and frequently came to play with Ashley at their house. When Stacey was a young girl, she was one of the few people who believed in him, when he was blamed by many people for losing Bradley. Being the eldest brother, he was held responsible for looking after the welfare of his little brother, particularly that day, out there, in the snow. People felt that he had been negligent and selfish in focusing on his own enjoyment and therefore, partly to blame for his brother's death. Stacey was present on one of those occasions when some of the villagers made a nasty comment to him. She ran towards him and deliberately walked by his side, slipping her arm under his and sticking her tongue out at them. She then turned to Tom and loudly proclaimed, 'Ignore them, Tom. They are just idiots.' He was grateful for her support and encouragement but pushed her arm away and walked off without looking back. Tom frequently felt guilty, when he thought back to those times and wished that he had not stopped being her friend. Ashley showed her hatred and resentment towards him after their brother was murdered, so he thought that it would be for the best to keep his distance from both of them.

Punton, being a small village, there was no getting away from bumping into people that one knew. Years later, after trying to avoid coming into close contact with Stacey, Tom came face to face with her. He could no longer resist her charms and from then on, they began a loving relationship together. They soon got married and it did not take too long before they decided that it would be nice to have a baby. After a year of trying, there was still no sign of Stacey becoming pregnant. They both went to see the doctor to seek advice and after a medical examination they were told that Tom was impotent. Stacey told him that it did not matter because they still had one another and it was enough for her. Tom knew that Stacey yearned to have a baby and yet after the doctor gave them the bad news, she never spoke of it again. He felt a great sense of remorse that he could not give her the very thing that she always wanted. Stacey on the other hand sensed how inadequate Tom felt as an alpha male. This made her all the more determined to make him feel that he was man enough for her. Tom knew this and he loved her even more for it. He felt like the luckiest man in the world to have a wife like her. Perhaps mostly because Stacey idolised him and that appealed to his very nature. He loved to have control.

When Tom could no longer keep up the mortgage payments for their five bedroom house due to living well above his means, they had to sell it and live with Tom's father. Again, Stacey accepted the situation without any resistance or complaint. There was no doubt in his mind that all Stacey cared about was that they were together. No man could be loved more ardently by his wife than he was.

Even though Stacey tried to hurry Tom to go to work, he was still dithering. 'Ashley is arriving around midday,' said Tom. He was feeling frustrated because of all the days for his sister to turn up, it had to be on the day that he would be later than ever back home. He had to meet a deadline on a project that he was working on.

'I know, I know, you told me a thousand times darling. Trust me, we will have a great natter. To think I am seeing your sister again after all this time. She was my best friend at school. I can't wait to meet her again.' Stacey grinned with enthusiasm.

'That is what I'm afraid of.' Tom muttered with complete sincerity.

Stacey giggled, finding what Tom had just said funny and lightly patted him on the chest, 'You know what happens when girls get together… go, before you are really late.'

Tom smiled and rushed out of the front door, turned to wave and then got into the car. As Stacey closed the front door, he paused and thoughtfully looked at the house. 'I hope you both don't say too much,' he mumbled to himself. Placing the key into the ignition, he started the car and drove off. Things were out of his hands now.

Tom would have to put his worst fears to the back of his mind for now, until he returned home.

*

Stacey closed the door behind her. The house always seemed empty without Tom being there. She knew that it was pointless to mope around as he had to go to work to earn the money and she had her chores to get on with. There was always plenty to do and especially since she started working again. After Tom had his pay cut, she decided to go back to work, just so that she could help a little with the finances. Unfortunately, she left school with only four G.C.S.E.'s and without any formal training towards a career. Stacey did not want to travel far to work; therefore, she was very happy when a vacancy arose at the local store. She wasted no time to apply for it and was accepted for the job as a cashier. Although the wages were poor, they still helped towards the bills and it made her feel good that she was making a contribution in some small way. Stacey always made herself available, whenever the opportunity arose, to work extra hours. The extra pay was handy and she was always keen to earn it. Being kept busy with work and the household chores was exhausting, but it made her feel content that she was doing everything possible to help her husband.

That day, Stacey took the day off in order to welcome Ashley home. At least it would be one less thing for Tom to worry about. She felt excitement bubble up inside her stomach, as she had not seen Ashley since she left Punton to go to University. At first they had sent lengthy letters to each other, then emails and the odd text or two. Finally, when Ashley moved to Australia, Stacey emailed her several times but never got a reply. Once she realised that her emails where being ignored, it saddened her immensely.

The one thing that Stacey could never really understand and it played on her mind was why Tom and Ashley had grown so far apart. They were so close once and there was a time when Ashley worshiped her brother. Stacey had no idea what could have caused the huge rift between them but whatever it was, must have been serious. Of course, the family had gone through a terrible tragedy but it should have brought the two of them even closer together.

Stacey realised that things deteriorated between Ashley and Tom just after poor Bradley was found dead. Before the tragic event, the two of them went everywhere together. Even though Tom was older, he was quite happy for Ashley to tag along with him and Adam. When it was term time at school, Tom occasionally placed a bar of chocolate into Ashley's coat pocket. When she found the chocolate, Ashley would share it with her. After school they always walked home with Tom and Adam and when the weather was hot, Tom would buy them an ice cream. That all stopped when Tom and Ashley returned to school after Bradley's funeral.

Stacey once asked her friend why Tom had stopped walking home with them after school. Ashley replied that she did not want to talk about it. The atmosphere turned frosty so Stacey decided never to broach the subject ever again.

During Mass, the two girls used to sit in the back pew together, pulling faces or nudging one another to see which one would be the first to start giggling. When the Davis family ceased going to church, Stacey had to sit with her parents and Mass became incredibly boring without her friend.

The following year, Tom moved to secondary school and the only time Stacey ever saw him was when he passed her on the road or happened to be in the shop at the same time as she was. It became obvious, that each time they met, he deliberately ignored her and as a result, Stacey gave up trying to talk to him. Tom clearly wanted nothing to do with her anymore, as if she was somehow entangled between the rift with him and his sister.

It came as a shock years later, when Tom and her accidently attended the same village dance. Not only did they start talking again but fell deeply in love. Revelling in this new, all-consuming relationship, Stacey decided not to dwell on the past events but to build on a new and happy future with Tom.

Ashley had by that time moved to Australia and it was clear that none of the family had any proper contact with her and she with them. Stacey accepted that her once best friend and Tom's sister would not return to Punton for the wedding. Stacey simply thought that Ashley made a new life for herself and was too busy or disinterested to make the flight for their big day.

Now that Ashley was returning from Australia to attend the funeral of Tom's old friend, Adam, she felt hurt. Of course, Adam's death was extremely horrific, especially since he had ended his own life in such a gruesome way but why bother to travel all that way for him and not for Tom and her best friend on their most important day? She had so many questions to ask Ashley and hoped that she could get some answers before Tom returned from work. She knew that digging up the past would only upset him, so having some time alone with Ashley, would give her the opportunity of finding out, once and for all, what really had happened to them both all those years ago.

Stacey looked at the clock. She had at least six hours before Ashley would arrive. This gave her enough time to prepare Ashley's old room and then drive to the nearest town to get the shopping. The village shop was sufficient for the daily needs but not as thrilling. Ashley could keep herself occupied before she faced her old friend. Even though she was excited, she was also nervous. Would they be able to revive their friendship and still get on as they used to before Ashley broke the ties between them? Stacey sincerely hoped so. She could not wish for anything better but to bring the three of them together again.

CHAPTER FIVE

Ashley chose to walk to her family home from the bus stop. She decided to stay in England for only two nights and return to what she now classed as home, Australia. Even though Ashley decided not to stay long, she crammed her large suitcase full of clothes, shoes, nightwear and toiletries, making it very heavy to pull. Ashley had never managed to master the art of travelling light, with only the things that she would need for the duration of her stay.

As she made her way by foot, the cool breeze swept over her face and blew her hair back. Ashley stopped moving for a few seconds to breathe in deeply, welcoming its icy touch. It refreshed her senses, allowing her to keep awake and restore the ability of rational thought.

As she walked along the main road, she looked around from left to right and noticed that Punton had not changed at all from the time she left. The houses and the quaint cottages remained unaltered, even their front doors stayed the same colour. She stopped and regarded the village pub across the road from where she was standing. It was a small, white building and yet the locals flocked inside and the sound of laughter and lively conversation could be heard coming from inside. It was the heart of the village where people could socialise during lunch times or the evenings and learn about the latest gossip. She smiled to herself as she remembered running into the pub when she was only six years old. It was out of bounds to children and therefore, her parents could not take her or Tom inside. Their father would bring them a packet of crisps and lemonade each and then go back in and join their mother and friends. Being a little girl with a lively imagination, she became curious to know what went on in there. The place took on an air of mystery and she would create her own vivid scenes of what happened inside the white building. These scenarios were very wild, extremely magical and at times quite disturbing. However, when she had charged through the door that day, she was disappointed to find that the room was filled with basic tables and chairs and looked very ordinary. It was nothing like something out of a fairytale book at all. There were men drinking beer and the women sipping shorts. They were all smoking cigarettes and as she stumbled in front of them, they gazed absently at her for a moment. Then, they turned back to each other and continued with their conversation. All the other customers further inside the room, including her parents, did not even notice her.

The landlord upon seeing her, quickly took her to the side and gently explained that the pub was for adults and that she must never come in again until she was older. Then he patted her gently on the head and sent her outside to the garden to play. Ashley shrugged her shoulders because the mystery was over. What she saw did not interest her at all. She no longer wanted to go into the pub.

As she continued to walk through the streets, she came across an alleyway that led to a small playing field. This was once her favourite hangout because it contained a huge slide, a number of multi-coloured swings and a roundabout. She would often spend her free time, looking up at the sky, while the roundabout slowly turned round and round. She sometimes went there with Stacey but preferred to be alone and drift off with her own thoughts.

One day, when she was ten years old, a group of older boys interrupted her daydreaming by finding it amusing to spin the roundabout again and again, faster and faster until she could no longer hold on to the bars. Her hands were not strong enough to maintain their grip. She flew off the roundabout, thumped her little body onto the ground and skidded across the gravel. Her forehead and knees were bleeding, the legs were badly grazed. Instead of helping her, the boys ran away leaving her sobbing on the ground, clutching her head. To this day, she still had a scar above her left eyebrow as a sharp stone cut into it deeply. She knew who the nasty lads were but chose not to reveal their identities. The pain soon faded but she never went back there on her own again.

Ashley was reminiscing over the past. The village once played a big part of her life but now Ashley felt that she no longer belonged there. She made a good life for herself in Australia and had no regrets that she had ever left. She was now convinced more than ever that she had made the right decision to flee all those years ago.

Ashley reached the front door of her old home and placing the bags on the step, knocked on the door. She expected her father to be the first one to welcome her with open arms, full of warmth and affection. As she waited, her heart began to beat with emotion and she imagined him to be now much older. Tears of joy would run down his cheeks at the sight of her. Both of them would just stand there for a few moments, embracing each other, as they used to when she was just a little girl.

She heard the rattle of the lock and raising her arms was ready to greet her father.

'Ashley, please come in. My goodness, it has been so long.' Stacey's voice was climbing to a high pitch with every word she said. There was a mixture of nervousness and excitement.

Confused, Ashley put her arms back down to her sides and asked, 'Where is my dad? And, who are you?'

'Well that's an awkward start.' Stacey rolled her eyes in an attempt to be humorous. 'It's me, Stacey. I know the years may not have been so kind but surely you must recognise me. You look great by the way.'

Ashley looked at her old friend and sighed, 'Of course I recognise you. It's just… well… I was not expecting you to be here. Where's my dad? Is he inside?'

Stacey stared at Ashley for a moment and in a more serious tone said, 'I guess you better come in. I think there are many things that I have to tell you. I'm not sure what you know and what you don't know. My goodness, I think this is going to be difficult.'

Ashley placed her bags on the corridor floor and made her way to the lounge. Stacey followed her quietly.

Instantly, Ashley noticed that the photographs on the sideboard of her parent's on their wedding day were gone. Instead they had been replaced by Tom and Stacey. One was of them standing by the Eiffel tower, grinning and holding hands. Another showed them by the beach, dressed in diving suits and giving the camera the thumbs up. She frowned and looked at Stacey questioningly.

'You do know that me and Tom are married, don't you?' Stacey was shocked to see Ashley's eyes widen by the news. 'I presumed you didn't want to come to our wedding. You were invited.'

'No-one told me.' Ashley sounded upset.

'I told Tom to ring you...' Stacey was too bewildered to complete the sentence.

'Well, he obviously didn't. What else is there that I should know about, Stacey? I need to know.' Ashley felt alarmed. She was uncertain as to what she would find out next.

'I think I better put the kettle on. Sit down, this may take some time.' Stacey whispered, unsure of where to start.

*

Stacey brought in two mugs of steaming hot coffee and a plate of biscuits. Ashley watched Stacey move around the house with confidence, as though she owned the place and this worried her.

'So, you and Tom. When did that happen?' Ashley opened up the conversation.

'We first got together at a village dance. It was just after you left for Australia. At the time, I never expected anything to come of it.' Stacey could not help but smile, shyly.

'You love him don't you?' Ashley murmured. It was not really a question but a comment. There was something sad in her voice, as if she pitied the woman sitting opposite her.

Stacey looked at her and nodded her head, 'Of course I do. Ashley, he is a good man. He's your brother for God's sake.' She paused for thought. 'Is it me? Are you upset that he married me?'

Ashley glanced at her friend and then took a sip of her coffee. She placed the mug on her lap, holding it tightly between both of her hands. She licked her lips and sat slightly more forward. 'Look, it's nothing against you. In normal circumstances, I would be pleased for my brother to marry the best friend I ever had at school.'

'Then what is it? Why did it come to this? Why do you hate Tom so much?' Stacey spluttered.

Ashley cautiously regarded Stacey. 'It's nothing really. We just grew apart. We got older and I moved away. It happens.'

Stacey was flummoxed and did not believe a word of what Ashley had said. 'That's rubbish and you know it. Something happened and neither of you will tell me what it was.'

'Have you asked Tom?' Ashley raised her voice.

Stacey shrunk back into her seat and quietly muttered, 'No.'

'Then don't say things that you don't understand. Anyway, I'm supposed to be asking the questions. Where the hell is my dad? Does he even know I'm back?' Ashley slammed the mug down on the side table. Droplets spilled over the top of the mug and splattered across it.

'Your dad? I thought you would know.' Stacey was puzzled. 'You don't know anything do you? Wait until Tom gets back. It's his place to tell you, not mine.'

'To hell with Tom! I want you to tell me now!' Ashley was losing her patience.

Stacey looked out of the window, wondering what to do. After a few moments, she turned back to Ashley and said, 'Do you remember how much your father changed after your mother was taken away? You were still here when he stopped working. He used to act as though he was lost. He could no longer get a grip of his life.' Stacey spoke softly.

'He wasn't that bad.' Ashley remained defiant.

'Well, he deteriorated when you left,' Stacey added.

Stacey was merely mimicking what Tom had told her. After Bradley's death she stopped going to Ashley's house and lost all contact with not only Tom but Mr Davis as well. It was not until she reached the age of twenty-four when Tom brought her to the house as his girlfriend that she was able to resume her relationship with Mr Davis again. Now more confident with sharing her own experiences she explained, 'When I married Tom, I could see that your father was unable to take care of himself and it became difficult for us to look after him. We were building our life together and it was better to place him in a care home. He seemed quite happy with the idea and chose the best one to reside in. Before long he agreed to let all of his assets to be transferred to Tom with a proviso that money from it would be deducted to pay for his care and some spending money for life. It helped us financially because Tom had to take a reduction in his wages. This is now our house and all the money that was in your father's bank belongs to us too.'

Ashley stared at Stacey, she had grown pale. It took her a few moments to process exactly what Stacey was telling her. 'You mean, Tom stole my inheritance. He convinced Dad to hand everything over to him whilst he sticks my father in some home to die? Isn't that illegal?'

'It wasn't quite like that Ashley, I promise. It was for the best. You weren't even here.' Stacey tried to keep things calm.

'And that gave you and Tom the right to make the decision without consulting me?' Ashley was furious. 'I can't believe this is even happening. I've heard just about enough for now. Firstly, I need to be alone, get some sleep. Then, when Tom gets back, I will to speak to him.'

'Don't be mad at him. He is under a lot of pressure at the moment.' Stacey panicked. She knew that she had said too much but was powerless to do anything about it now that things were said.

'He's my brother. I can say whatever I damn well want! Now, show me which room I am to stay in and leave me alone for a while.' Ashley stood up and made her way into the corridor. She waited by the stairs for Stacey to take the lead. She had a thumping headache and wanted to be strong for when she confronted Tom.

Silently, Stacey gave a cumbersome smile and picking up Ashley's bags, began to walk up the stairs.

CHAPTER SIX

James was released from prison only six days ago and yet he was already starting to piece his life back together again. Each step that James took was a small one but nevertheless a positive one forward. He knew from the onset that it would not be easy but he was determined to make it work.

It was Thursday evening and he had just finished his shift at the large supermarket in town. His feet ached from standing all day. He sat on the hard, single bed and took off his shoes. He gazed out of the window and thought back to the first day of his release.

After seeing Anna on that Saturday, James spent the rest of the day trying to find somewhere to live. He knew that it would be pointless to try in Punton because the locals would more than likely attempt to arrange a lynch squad than welcome him back into the community. James did not blame them for that because as far as they were concerned, he murdered their little, lovable, local boy, Bradley. However, he was determined to stay as close to Punton as possible so that if his children agreed to see him, he would be close enough to meet them before they changed their minds. With this thought, he took a long walk to the next village to try his luck there but he was met with the same kind of animosity. The first five landlords recognised him immediately and each door was slammed in his face together with some verbal abuse. One of them even spat in his face. James was getting to the point of giving up searching and coming to terms with the possibility of spending the night sleeping on a park bench, when, as if by some chance, he came across a notice board advertising vacant rooms to rent at a Victorian town house in Selby Road. When James scribbled the landlord's address on the back of his hand, he noticed that it was different from the one he was hoping to rent. The address of the landlord was familiar to him because many years ago, when he and Anna were about to get married, it was one of a few villages that they considered buying a house. He remembered the quaint cottage because they both fell in love with its charm and beauty at the time, therefore, it would be relatively easy for him to find. Within half an hour he was already standing on the doorstep, bracing himself to knock on the door and having it slammed in his face as he already experienced with the others. He took a deep breath and rapped on the door three times with the large iron knocker. It made a loud thudding noise that seemed far too loud for such a quiet environment. He waited for a few moments and then heard someone turning the knob. The door opened slowly, creaking loudly on its rusty hinges.

A small, chubby old lady with pale blue eyes finally emerged, staring at him out of curiosity and then said, 'Yes?' Her voice was weak but very gentle. James felt a glimmer of hope upon hearing that sweet, soft voice. She had only said one word and yet he instantly warmed to the frail lady.

'I'm sorry to bother you but I noticed that you have rooms to let in your Victorian house in Selby Road. I was hoping, if I could rent one of them.' James tried to sound as polite as possible in fear of frightening her.

'Of course dear. Do come inside and I will get my husband. He deals with all this kind of thing.' She smiled brightly and gestured for him to enter.

James was shocked. She actually did not recognise him. Feeling a bit less anxious, he stepped across the threshold. The narrow corridor led to a small sitting room. There was very little light coming in from the tiny window and the colour scheme of the room was dark. The carpet was brown with navy blue and mustard flowery patterns. The wallpaper was also floral and of similar shades as the carpet. All of the furniture was old, tired and dated. However, there was something welcoming and friendly about the place.

'George is in the garden. I won't be a moment. Please, do sit down.' She pointed to the sofa and slowly made her way to the back door.

James noticed some photographs on the sideboard and decided to take a closer look at them. There was an old black and white one of a young man and woman. They were standing outside a church door. The woman wore a plain wedding dress and clutched a small bouquet of flowers in her hands. She was extremely pretty. The man stood upright, straight backed and beamed with pride. He held the woman gently around the waist as if he was holding a delicate piece of china. James realised that the picture was of the lady that he had just met and obviously her husband. They looked so content and excited to be starting their lives together. James remembered feeling like that once and bowed his head in sorrow.

Scanning through the line of photographs, James could see that each one was taken during important events in their lives. One showed the same couple holding a small baby. The next snapshot was in colour of a young girl, obviously their daughter, posing in a tutu, holding a trophy. Then next one was of a couple who were now older, standing proudly next to their daughter who was holding their grandchild. A young man of the same age as the daughter was standing next to them, looking lovingly towards them. James found it fascinating, how the pictures captured and told the story of three generations. It was heart-warming to see the photographs displaying their happiness as a family. He would have done anything to have shared that kind of love and devotion with his wife and children.

'So, you want to rent a room?' A voice just as weak and gentle as the woman's startled James, bringing him back to reality. He turned to see a short man who was as chubby as his wife, leaning on a walking stick. He too had a sweet smile like his wife and James could see from this that they were a perfect match. 'Would you like to see it now?' The man held up a set of keys.

'No, it won't be necessary.' James was prepared to rent the room no matter what condition it was in. He was desperate to find somewhere to stay and did not care what it looked like. He just needed a bed and roof over his head and that would make him feel content.

'Okay. It's not much but has the basic necessities. There is a communal bathroom shared by three other tenants. We charge £300 a month,' George explained. 'No pets, no changes to be made to the room unless you ask our permission. The post is left on a table by the front door.'

James knew that it would not be easy what he was about to say next to the landlord. He would have to find a way that would not evoke any suspicion as to his predicament or having to answer awkward questions. Feeling very tense and nervous, James began saying, slowly with a stutter, 'I am very sorry but I um, can't pay any money in advance because I um, have not got a job as yet. I do promise you, that I will try to find one immediately.' He felt his voice trembling and face burning but was hopeful that the lovely couple would allow him at least one week's grace. He already found it a miracle that they did not know who he was and prayed that he could continue to keep his identity a secret from them.

George abruptly interrupted, 'Lily could you get the contract out of the drawer for me.' He then turned to look at James, staring straight into his eyes, making him feel even more uncomfortable. 'I am fully aware of your situation, Mr Dickson as you were only released this morning. We will start taking payment from you in one month. That should give you enough time to find your feet, so to speak. I think you will find that the contract is rather standard.'

James was lost for words.

'I will get you a few things from the kitchen cupboard to take with you. I am sure that you will be short of food for a while.' Lily had just returned from the drawer with the contract in one hand and a pen in the other. She held them both out for James to sign.

'Are you sure? I thought you didn't recognise me.' James could hardly speak. He was overwhelmed by their generosity.

'We are just old dear, not clueless,' Lily laughed lightly. 'Besides everyone deserves a chance.'

'You served your time. It's not for us to judge.' George added.

As James left the cottage with the keys and a huge bag of food and toiletries, he turned to the couple and thanked them profusely for their kindness, 'I just want to assure you that I am innocent. I will do my utmost to prove it.'

George smiled and extended his hand out to him, 'You still stick by that don't you? Well, I wish you every success.'

James took George's hand and shook it, smiled and then walked away.

After experiencing such warmth, it was time, once more, to be met with dirty looks and frosty receptions. For a brief moment, he felt human again and for that, he would be eternally grateful.

Finding a job proved even harder. It seemed that no-one wanted to employ him. He tried various places without being fussy about the nature of the work but he was refused each time. As a last resort, he went to ask for a job at a supermarket in a town that was the nearest to the village. Being short staffed, they were keen to take him on. He was placed on the delicatessen counter where he would serve cheese, cooked meats, various pies and quiches.

Today had been his first day and it was not as simple as he expected it to be. Some of the customers made nasty comments to his face while others walked off and muttered under their breath. In truth, James could not blame them. He would have done the same if he was in their place.

One person, who caught his attention that day, was an attractive, young lady who was so enveloped in her own shopping that she barely looked at him. She had placed a fair amount of items in her trolley and appeared rather excitable.

'I have an old friend coming to stay. Haven't seen her in years,' she chirped as she scanned the length of the counter.

'Well, then you must buy something special.' James grew in confidence because she treated him just like any other ordinary Deli shop assistant.

'Indeed! What do you suggest?' She appeared to lift her face to look at him but in fact gazed through him as though too preoccupied with her own thoughts.

'Can I suggest a platter of different meats, cheeses and things? The bread counter has got some amazingly good bread. I can smell it from here.' James began to offer her some advice.

'Good idea. She is travelling from Australia so I shouldn't think that she will want a huge, sit down meal. You know what journeys can be like. Jet lag and all that.'

The woman smiled showing a perfectly straight set of teeth.

Nodding, James began to pick out what he felt were the best items from the goods before him. 'How much would madam like?'

'I never thought of that. Shall we say eight slices of each, please?' Stacey gave a pained expression. She was not certain if that would be enough for all of them.

'Sounds like a good, rounded number to me,' James chuckled. He was enjoying this little conversation. It did not take him long to weigh and bag all the items and felt sad, that soon, she would be walking away. 'Well, that's everything Miss…'

'Mrs Davis,' she replied.

Hearing the name froze James to the core. The boy, who he was accused of murdering, was a Davis. Was it just a coincidence or was this woman some kind of relative?

'And what is your name?' she asked politely as she packed the goods into the trolley. 'It would be nice to know the name of the gentleman who will be serving me on this counter from now on. You're new aren't you?' Even though Stacey appeared to take a quick glimpse of him a few times, she was far too preoccupied to pay any real attention as to what he really looked like.

James was unsure of what to say. His mind went totally blank and before he could make up a name for himself, he blurted out, 'James.'

'Well, James, I am sure that I will be seeing you again soon. Thanks for your suggestions.' After that, she hastily made her way to the bread counter.

James watched her as she walked away, pushing her trolley. Then, he suddenly remembered that the family had an elder son; could she have married him? He had the rest of the day to ponder over it. James truly hoped that she was the older brother's wife because this could possibly give him the opportunity of explaining to the family that he was not responsible for the poor boy's death. They deserved to know the truth. He hoped, the next time she came into the supermarket, he could discreetly ask her without giving himself away. He doubted that the boy's immediate family would ever want to talk to him but maybe she would give him a chance to explain.

As James was sitting on the bed, contemplating over the day's events, looking around at the gloomy and rundown room, the telephone on the side table began to ring, disrupting his thoughts.

When he found the room, James called Anna straight away to give her the telephone number, so that she would pass it on to the children. Perhaps they would call to make arrangements to meet him.

James felt a tingle crawl up his back and the blood drain from his face. He quickly reached across the bed to pick up the receiver and said, 'Hello.'

For a moment there was silence and James repeated, 'Hello.'

'Um… Hi… It's Eloise,' she said in a well-spoken voice. James closed his tearful eyes as a rush of joy filled his whole being. He was hearing the voice of his youngest daughter. This was the moment that he was longing and hoping for after waiting for so many years to hear it. She had been only eleven months when he last saw her. Now, she was a grown woman of thirty.

'Eloise, thank you for calling me, I…'

'Stop right there, please,' she asked, without any sign of agitation in her voice. 'I would rather talk face to face. I hate telephones and mobile phones, especially texting. It feels too impersonal for an important conversation. So, could we arrange to meet?'

James was ecstatic about this because it was something that he was yearning for. Her reaction towards him was positive and he could hardly contain his emotion. James quickly replied, 'Yes of course. I can meet up now if you like.'

'Tomorrow would suit better. How about the pub?' she returned.

'In Punton?' James was reluctant to meet there. He would have preferred somewhere less local. His presence would only cause trouble and destroy their reunion.

'Yeah, is there any problem?' Eloise sounded a little disappointed.

'No… no problem at all,' James instantly replied.

'Great, say 7 pm? Bye.' Before James could reply, she ended the call abruptly.

James placed the receiver back on the stand and just sat there staring at the phone. He could not believe that he was finally going to see his daughter again. At that moment, he had no idea what he was feeling. Was it relief, gratitude, fear? The only thing that he was sure about was to tell his daughter he loved her beyond anything and convince her that he is innocent.

CHAPTER SEVEN

Father Aiden stood with his back to the altar, looking down the aisle. It was Friday morning and even though the air was chilly, the sun was so intense, that its beams of white light pierced through the stained glass windows. The various colours on the floor formed beautiful patterns and specks of dust danced lazily in the air. It gave the whole place an ethereal atmosphere and brought the room to life. There was total silence inside the church and under any other circumstances, would have been perfect for a moment of peaceful reflection and undisturbed prayer. However, in less than half an hour, the mourners would be arriving to pay their last respects to the young man from Punton who took his own life.

Closing his eyes, Father Aiden could still see the bloody image in his mind; the head tilting slightly sideways to reveal a glassy eye. In a perverted sort of way, the eye looked very similar to that of a fish, displayed on the counter of the local fishmonger where Father Aiden made a purchase on a regular basis. Instead of crushed ice, the head lay on the small, wooden table. Oozing out from the nostrils with the pencils lodged inside, was the remains of thick, clotted, dark red blood that dripped off the edge of the table and splashed into the crimson pool on the floor. With sickening speed, the pool grew in circumference, maintaining a perfect circle. Both arms flopped on either side of the table, palms down and fingers splayed limply.

It was this image, that every night, formed Father Aiden's nightmares since the day he witnessed the suicide. It tore out his ability to sleep and shredded his brain so that he could no longer think clearly. Simple daily activities became impossible to manage and the once vibrant priest became quiet and withdrawn. Guilt engulfed Father Aiden because he felt the heavy load of blame on his shoulders for the poor man's death. Remorse lay on his chest like a heavy cloth, twisting tighter and tighter until there was no air left in his lungs to breath. Father Aiden questioned his ability of keeping his position as a priest as he went through the whole scene over and over again, step by step in his mind. Could he have prevented Adam from committing suicide? He did see the signs of a deeply troubled soul but did nothing to soothe it. He allowed Miss Colson to drone on instead of paying more attention to a man in desperate need of help. Adam had come to him for guidance and help and yet he sent him away to wait and then ignored him when he disobeyed his command. Was it his inexperience as a priest that pushed this man over the edge? Was it the fact that Miss Colson kept going on about Bradley and how his murderer was a monster? It must have been torture for Adam to hear it. Perhaps, because he was already being tormented by something, it might have added to his problem, knowing that he was partly responsible for losing the little boy in the first place and tipped him over the edge. Father Aiden knew that all this was simply supposition and maybe he was being unfair by pushing the blame of Adam's death onto Miss Colson, away from himself. The fact remained that if he had done things differently, and gave his total attention and support for Adam when he most needed it, then he might have been still alive today. He hated himself for letting Adam and the whole village down. Nevertheless, although he questioned his vocation, he still remained as the priest of Punton church. He failed to save Adam but he would be there to guide the mourners through this harrowing time. Father Aiden also feared that if he did not keep busy, the shocking business would eventually devour and destroy him.

He wondered how Miss Colson was dealing with it all. She was a very strong woman but had not stepped inside the church since that morning. No-one had seen or spoken to her since that day. Her friends and neighbours knocked on her door and peered through the windows fearing the worst. There was no sign of her to be seen. Father Aiden did hear whispers from some of the volunteers who cleaned the church, speculating that she had gone to stay with her sister in London, whilst others enjoyed a more morbid scenario. What started as the poor woman locking her door and remaining alone in her house, soon changed to her roaming around the rooms in her nightgown, carrying a torch in her hand in the dark. The more callous members of the parish changed the torch into a carving knife. These stories grew more sinister by the day.

Father Aiden knew that he too should have checked on her, rather than listen to silly gossip of her whereabouts. Even though she was a constant pain, now that she had disappeared, Father Aiden realised how much he was missing her company.

Slowly, Father Aiden moved towards the sacristy where he knelt and prayed for the sad loss of Adam Bradshaw and to strengthen his family and friends who were grieving at this difficult time. He also spared five minutes to pray for Miss Colson to have the power to get through the heart-rending incident.

*

The church was filling up with people. Father Aiden peeped out from the sacristy door to see some familiar faces as well as many who he had never seen before. At the front sat Adam's close relatives. His mother looked completely in ruins. No parent expects their child to die before them, especially when it's under such tragic circumstances. There could be no doubt that she was blaming herself for this. Mothers always do when something goes terribly wrong with their child's life. She would have constantly questioned herself after given the bad news. Perhaps, she did not give him enough of her time or something was lacking in his life that she failed to give? Could she somehow have prevented this from happening? Parents have a habit of torturing and blaming themselves when things go wrong when in fact it has nothing to do with them at all. So, here she was, standing in the front pew, close to the coffin, trembling and bending forward, slightly rocking back and forth as if uneasy on her feet whilst her husband held her tightly with one hand and rubbed her back with the other in a feeble attempt to console her. He too, looked broken. His sad, tear stained eyes were red and his face was pale and gaunt. Along the same row were unfamiliar faces so Father Aiden assumed that they were relatives that did not live in the village. They too, sat still with solemn faces.

Behind them, in the next three rows, were many of the congregation that attended Mass each week. The rest of the pews were taken by other members of the village who knew the deceased in one way or another. Each face was full of sorrow and disbelief as they stared at the coffin with red roses arranged in the shape of a cross, placed on the top. Adam's death affected the lives of many people. He had been such a popular, good natured soul.

Suddenly the back door opened and Father Aiden was pleased to see that Miss Colson had entered. Her whole demeanour expressed fatigue but she was meticulously dressed and showed no signs of madness. She looked quickly around at the people staring at her, before she quietly settled herself in one of the pews. Father Aiden looked pleased and decided that after the funeral, he would make sure that he would have a chat with her before she left.

After the opening hymn, Father Aiden began the Requiem Mass with a prayer. The congregation were silent and listened intently to Father Aiden's every word. He had led a few funerals before and yet the atmosphere in this one was a combination of tension and respect. Distress was clear on each person's face as they bowed their heads in private thought.

Two members of the family took responsibility for the readings. The bidding prayers were led by Tom, who was reluctant to do them at first but gave in to the grieving mother's request. Adam's father bravely managed to write and read the eulogy. His every word was spoken with great emotion that there was barely a dry eye in the room. He spoke proudly of Adam as a wonderful son and of his commitments to the community and achievements throughout his short life. At times, he paused to compose himself which filled each heart in the church with warmth and admiration for his bravery. This was the pure, true love of a father who was struggling within the depths of despair in order to honour his son.

It was soon time for the Sacrament of Holy Communion and then finally, the last hymn, before the coffin was carried by the bearers to its final resting place in the church grounds. Following behind the dark oak coffin, were the parents, the rest of the family and last of all, the remaining congregation. The sun shone brightly as though God himself was present in blessing each person and welcoming the departed soul into heaven.

As the coffin was lowered into the ground, a robin that had watched from a nearby tree began to chirp as if singing its own hymn of farewell, then flew into a bush.

When all had ended, some people began to discreetly make their way quietly home after giving their condolences to the family. Father Aiden had been invited to the wake but graciously declined. Everyone knew that he had witnessed Adam's last moments and this made him feel all the more ill at ease.

When everyone had left, there was only Father Aiden and Miss Colson standing by the grave.

'Would you please come in for a coffee?' asked Father Aiden.

'To be honest Father, I think I would like something much stronger right now. What about the whisky you keep hidden in the back of the kitchen cupboard?' she replied in her nasal, high pitched voice.

Instead of being irritated, her abrupt honesty humoured him. His smile widened and he chuckled, 'Nothing gets past you does it?'

'I am just thorough in my cleaning.' Miss Colson retorted even though she too broke into a smile. 'It's amazing what you can find when you clean every nook and cranny. You are a man of the cloth so I cannot tell you what various items I have found down settees and in cupboards over the years. It keeps things interesting, believe me.'

'I can imagine.' Father Aiden mused. 'May I please ask, where have you been all this time Miss Colson?'

With a more serious expression, Miss Colson replied, 'I have a friend in the next village up. She invited me to stay for a while and I gladly accepted her offer. I needed time to get myself together, just in the same way you did, I imagine. I'm back as from today; therefore, I can resume my duties at church.' She paused and then stared at Father Aiden, taking in his dull eyes and sullen expression. She noticed how drawn he had become in just those few, short days. 'You can't let anything get you down for too long Father. Wallow in self-pity and it will eventually eat you up. Besides, life is just too short. Anyway, I should not have left you in the lurch. I don't know how you coped without me.' After saying this, she started to walk towards the house.

Father Aiden gazed at her as she strolled briskly over the damp grass. 'Indeed, what would I do without you?' He shook his head in wonder by this strange yet incredible old lady.

CHAPTER EIGHT

After Adam's body was laid to rest at the cemetery, family and close friends were invited to the wake which was held at Mr and Mrs Bradshaw's house. Neither Tom nor Ashley wanted to attend but they felt that it would be unforgivable and impolite not to show their respect towards the bereaving family for at least a little while. Stacey was another reason why Tom felt obliged to go. She was determined to be present at the whole ritual and would not hear of missing the wake. Tom was not going to allow her to go on her own because it would spark off gossip around the village and he did not need any negative attention in such a small place. He enjoyed to live a quiet existence and in keeping his private life to himself, avoiding at all cost being the cause of any speculation from the public.

When Tom and Ashley arrived, they took a glass of sherry each from the table and decided to stand in the corner of the corridor, away from the other people while Stacey mingled with the family and guests. Tom watched as they chatted in small groups, many of whom were holding paper plates piled high with food from the buffet.

Here and there, he could hear snippets of conversation. One large, middle aged woman was commenting in a loud voice with her mouth full how the spread on the table was delicious and beautifully arranged. Those around her blinked and covered their plates with their hands as bits of food flew out of her mouth with every word that she said. Further to the left of where Tom was standing, an elderly gentleman was saying how sad he was because he could no longer grow the impressive tomatoes and cucumbers that constantly won him awards after he dismantled his old greenhouse the year before. No matter which conversation Tom chose to eavesdrop on, it had nothing at all to do with the funeral or the deceased.

Suddenly, Ashley turned her head around towards Tom and mumbled, 'I can't believe you did the bidding prayers, Tom. How hypocritical can you get?'

Tom shot his sister a frosty look. Even though no-one was paying any attention to them, Ashley was never good at whispering. This made Tom feel very uneasy.

'Keep your voice down will you?' Tom leaned close to Ashley with his lips almost touching the side of her face. As he spoke, Ashley's hair moved with the force of his breath. 'I did it because I was asked to.'

Ashley took a step away from Tom and took a sip of her drink. Before completely removing the glass from her mouth, she muttered, 'You stopped being Adam's friend when you were ten, for God's sake.'

'He stopped being my friend, remember?' Tom quipped.

'And whose fault was that?' replied Ashley.

'Stop it! We will talk about this later,' Tom growled.

'Is there any point?' Ashley had to have the last word.

Stacey watched the two of them from the kitchen, where she was filling her glass with more wine. She could not believe just how deeply they resented each other.

When Tom returned from work yesterday, Stacey could feel the immediate tension between him and Ashley. After not seeing each other for so many years, Stacey expected them to greet one another with hugs and kisses but instead they stared and kept at a distance. Every word that they spoke was clipped with animosity. This made it impossible to hold any form of civil conversation. The atmosphere was explosive so Stacey felt that it would be for the best to leave them alone together and retire to bed.

Of course, there was no chance of getting any sleep as she could hear their raised voices coming up through the floorboards. She tried to catch what they were saying but their words were muffled and incoherent. She presumed that they must have been bickering about their father's assets and how Tom had inherited everything. When Stacey told Ashley about the news before Tom came home from work, it made her very angry and sore. Ashley accused Tom of manipulating their father into leaving him everything and stealing her share of the inheritance. Stacey knew that this was not true. Tom would never have done that. It was entirely his father's decision but it would be difficult to prove this to Ashley.

After almost an hour, a door slammed and all went quiet. Stacey could hear someone stomping up the stairs. When a door slammed across the corridor, she realised that it was Ashley. Obviously, the heated argument had not helped to heal any rifts between the brother and sister.

This saddened her greatly, as too many times over the years, she had witnessed some of her own family members pulled apart by petty disagreements. Good relationships were often torn to shreds and those involved in them became bitter and twisted to the extent that their family ties would be severed forever. Stacey felt that family was the most important part in a person's life and after witnessing irreversible discord in her own family was scared that this would happen between Tom and Ashley.

A moment later, a second set of feet trudged up the stairs. Stacey felt slightly nervous knowing that Tom would be entering the bedroom. She knew that she had done the wrong thing by telling Ashley far too much. It would have been better if she had left it to Tom's discretion. It was his sister after all. On top of that, he was not in the best of moods. He would be exhausted from the long day at meetings as well as the tedious drive home.

The door slowly opened and she could hear Tom shuffle across the deep piled carpet to her side of the bed. He had not put the main light on and Stacey suspected that he did not want to disturb her if she was sleeping. Anyway, she could not see him as she was facing the other way. For a moment there was silence; then he kissed her gently on the cheek and quietly said, 'I love you.'

Hearing this, Stacey turned towards him and replied, 'Love you too.'

Tom was surprised and sat on the edge of the bed. 'Thought you were asleep.'

Stacey leaned across and switched the side light on. Pushing her hair away from her face, she smiled at her husband pitifully. 'Bit impossible to.'

Tom rubbed his forehead with irritation. 'Sorry about that. She can be very difficult at times. At least she goes back on Saturday so we won't have to put up with her for long.'

'Tom, I was just thinking about that. It's been years since you last saw her. This could be an opportunity for you both to sort things out.'

'There is nothing to sort out,' Tom fired back, defensively.

'I'm not stupid. I can see there are some unresolved things between you. Ask her to stay longer.' Stacey reached out her hand to gently stroke Tom's hair.

Tom took hold of her hand and kissed it. 'You always have my best interests at heart, don't you?' He smiled sorrowfully and continued, 'I'll try, but only because you want me to. I can't promise that she will and I definitely can't promise that things will be great between my sister and me. Now go to sleep, it's getting late.' He stood up. 'We have got a funeral to go to tomorrow.'

'Tom?' Stacey stopped him from going to the bathroom. 'I'm sorry if I said too much to Ashley.'

'It's not your fault honey.' Tom replied tenderly, giving Stacey a wink at the same time and then headed towards the bathroom.

Now, here she was at the wake, staring at the two of them huddled in the corridor. One of Adam's aunties was jabbering on about something to her but Stacey was not listening. Rather offhandedly she remarked, 'Excuse me.' Without as much as a glance at the woman she went over to Tom and Ashley.

As she approached, Tom's face softened and he held out his arm ready to embrace her. Gladly, she slid up to his side and pressed her hand against his chest whilst holding him tightly around the waist with her other arm. She smiled broadly at Ashley and said in a soft voice, 'Are you okay?'

Ashley forced a smile in return and replied ironically, 'As good as can be expected, considering we are at a funeral.'

'Of course,' answered Stacey politely and then asked, 'has Tom managed to ask you something?'

Ashley frowned and looked up at her brother.

'Not yet,' Tom interjected. 'We were wondering if you would like to stay longer with us. I am sure that your school gave you more than three days off and well…'

Before Tom could finish his sentence, Adam's father interrupted him by saying, 'So glad you could make it today, Ashley and thanks Tom for saying the bidding prayers. That was very good of you. My wife and I truly appreciate it and we know that Adam would have too. I hope you both won't mind but I have something to show you. It's something I think you should both see.' He turned to look at Stacey who had let go of Tom and was already prepared to be left behind. 'Pardon me Stacey, of course you can come with us as well.'

Stacey felt that she was not really wanted and so shook her head and remarked, 'No, its fine John. Obviously, this concerns Tom and Ashley, so I'll stay here and get to know more of your family.'

'Good. That would be nice.' John gave a thankful smile and said, 'Please, follow me.' He then turned towards the stairs and started to slowly make his way up. Tom kissed Ashley on the cheek, shrugged his shoulders and followed quietly. Ashley walked behind them.

John stopped by a door and took out a key. He placed it in the lock and turned it until it clicked. He paused for a moment and then opened the door. A slight, musky aroma wafted out from inside the dark room. Tom and Ashley realised that this must have been Adam's old room before he left home. The curtains were drawn as a sign of respect for him. John switched the light on as he entered it. He beckoned them both to enter and proceeded to a chest of drawers.

Both Tom and Ashley noticed that a white sheet covered the mirror on top of the drawers. Clearly, John took the traditional style of mourning and was thorough in following the Victorian etiquette.

He opened the top drawer and took out what seemed an expensive black leather case. On closer inspection, Tom could see that it was in fact a luxury notepad. Neither of them said a word, they just watched as John carefully brought it to them.

'I found this in Adam's flat when I was clearing it out.' John gently brushed one hand over its cover. 'It is a sort of scrapbook that he kept.'

Both Tom and Ashley remained silent but stared intently at the pad in John's possession.

'Once I found it, I did not want anyone else to see it, so, I have kept it hidden here ever since. You must promise me that once you look over it, you will keep it a secret and tell no-one about it.'

Tom and Ashley nodded in unison and their curiosity made them impatient to take a look inside. Adam's father created such a crescendo that they could barely resist the urge to swipe the scrapbook from his hands.

They were not the only ones hypnotised by John Bradshaw's words. Jeremy, the small local farm owner had just come out of the lavatory and noticed that the bedroom door was wide open. He knew that when he first came up the stairs, it had been shut. Quietly, he tiptoed closer to listen in on the conversation. He was intrigued by the whole thing.

Ashley took the book from John and opened it on the first page. Slowly, she flicked through the next three pages as Tom leaned over her shoulder to get a good view as well. There were several clippings about Bradley's death as well as some that followed James Dickson's court case up to the point when he was sentenced to life imprisonment. It made the two of them shiver when they saw, scrawled across the article, 'NOT GUILTY'. They paused over this for a moment and then Tom stretched his arm across Ashley and turned the page over.

'I too, was surprised at first, when I saw that.' John commented sadly.

Neither Tom nor Ashley responded to this and so his words were left hanging in the air.

Then, the clippings became disturbing. It appeared that Adam had become obsessed with anyone who had been buried alive in snow. One was of a case at an Idaho ski resort where three children had been buried under seven feet of falling snow. The youngest, a two year old girl tragically died. The other two, both girls aged seven, were revived at the scene.

Another article told of how a man in New Hampshire survived after being buried under snow for more than 3 hours. He said at first he couldn't move but the snow above his head melted to the point where it created a 4 to 5 inch hole in the snow, allowing him to breath. Once he was found, it took the emergency crews about 20 minutes to dig him out.

There were so many other articles from Poland, Russia and France, which were some of the countries that suffered with heavy snowfall.

Ashley read one more article while Tom frowned over her shoulder. In New York, two children were hidden under snow for hours. She had been drawn to that article because the ages, times and the word '*hours*' were all underlined, circled or highlighted. They left home at 6 pm. The police were called at 10 pm. They were found at 2 am.

Adam had made a guess of how many hours they had remained trapped. In the margin was written, '*Possibly seven hours!*'

They miraculously survived.

Flicking through the pages, it became evident that all the children's ages, and the times of the events were underlined with a thick pencil or highlighter pen. Tom, finally spoke, 'God, so much time went into this. He must have searched for the articles to find out about children who were buried in snow. What was going on in his mind?'

Ashley flashed Tom a strange look. It was missed by John because he had his head bent down towards the floor.

'I think you can see why I don't want too many people knowing about this,' John muttered. 'My poor son must have suffered with the guilt of losing Bradley that day. If you look closely, he focuses on the survivors. It's as if he wished that Bradley had survived and this in time drove him to suicide. I should have seen it coming.' John's voice began to break as he said this and all of a sudden he burst out crying. He shook uncontrollably with the force of the emotion that was growing inside of him and finally erupting from the core of his being. He was consumed by guilt. He entirely blamed himself for missing the signs, that his only son was treading the thin wire of an unbalanced mind. Without crying for help or seeking solace, Adam was eventually tipped over the edge and fell into the dark pit of death. John found this impossible to bear. He felt that he let his son down and yet in reality there was nothing that he could have done. Adam seemingly carried on with his life, while in reality carried the burden of guilt on his shoulders, resulting in his demise.

Ashley closed the book and placed it gently on the bed. She and Tom stood still, side by side like statues, not knowing what to do next.

John struggled to compose himself but once he managed to pull himself together he quickly apologised for his outburst. He picked up the scrapbook from the bed and placed it back into the drawer. 'The only thing I can't understand is that he never blamed the murderer. It was proved in the court of law that James was the killer. Yet,

Adam never judged him or hated him. It was as though he took the burden of responsibility onto himself. It all seems so strange.'

Suddenly the room felt claustrophobic and Tom no longer wanted to stay in it. 'Think we should go.'

Ashley moved towards John and soothingly said, 'Thank you for sharing this with us. We won't breathe a word. You can rely on us to do that. But why did you feel that we should see this?'

John looked up and gave a wistful smile. 'Adam has always held your family in high regards. He never stopped liking you. He often spoke of you and Tom. If you both had not been his friends back then, I am sure that he would not have had any other. He was not like the other kids; Adam was a gentle, sweet soul. He particularly adored Bradley and took his death very hard. I wanted you to see that for yourselves.'

They did not notice, all this time, that Jeremy was standing by the bedroom door and hastily slipped away and quickly descended the stairs, once they were ready to leave.

'Come on, let's go back downstairs.' Tom had become pale and felt damp along the collar of his shirt. He needed some fresh air. He took Ashley's arm and pulled her towards the door. Reluctantly, she followed. As the two of them moved down the stairs they could hear John locking the bedroom door behind him.

Stacey was standing in the same place as when they left her. Taking her glass from her hands, Tom emphatically said, 'I want to leave now.'

A bewildered Stacey followed him as he made his way to the front door. She turned to Ashley and raised her eyebrows, questioningly.

'I'll tell you everything later,' was all Ashley could say.

CHAPTER NINE

James cautiously entered the pub through the back door. He tried to make himself as obscure as possible. He knew that this was the worst place for him to meet his daughter, especially since it was the evening of Adam's funeral. He had heard various villagers whisper speculations as they pondered the fact that James' release from prison was on the same day that Adam took his own life. Of course, it could have all been just a strange coincidence but when you include a convicted murderer into the equation, everything becomes all the more sinister. The wake had ended long ago but the hard-core drinkers would have automatically reunited here and settled for the rest of the evening. James was sure that he was the most hated man in the world right now and was the last person that the villagers would want to clap their eyes on. Emotions were high and tempers would flare easily. By walking into this particular pub, James was putting himself into a risky position of being physically shredded to pieces but he was desperate to see his little girl. His impending relationship with her was at a delicate stage right now and he had no choice but to obey her commands. If this was the place she chose to meet, then so be it.

James stopped in the corridor that led to the main lounge and surveyed the room from the shadows. It was packed with people, mostly male, dressed in black attire. Occasionally, a few words were mumbled but the conversation appeared to be slow and apathetic. Many had their heads bowed over pints of beer. The smell of alcohol was intoxicating and nauseous as it was mixed with the cigarette smoke that came in through the open window. The room itself was far too small to fit so many people in, which contributed to the extremely stifling air inside.

Noticing a vacant, corner table, James pulled down his cap in an attempt to hide his face and then entered the room. He walked up to the bar and almost inaudibly asked for a pint of bitter. He pulled some change out of his jacket pocket and paid for his drink. He did not recognise the man serving behind the bar which was of great relief to him. He half expected to be told to leave by Simon who was the landlord of the pub, now thirty years ago. Of course, he should have realised that there would be a new landlord because that would make Simon about ninety. He would have either retired or died.

As the bartender placed the pint in front of James, he whispered, 'You got a nerve being in here... of all days.'

James looked up at the man who was leaning closely towards him. His expression was stern and his eyes cold. James stared at him intently and then realised that there was something familiar about the shape of his eyes and the thickness of the eyebrows. 'Jacob?' James asked gently. 'It can't be. I used to give you sweets when you were just a lad. You were always playing on the swing in the pub garden, even when it rained.' He was so engrossed momentarily with reminiscing over the past, that he almost forgot the awkward position he was in.

Simon had been very strict about the rules of the establishment. A huge sign hung on the outside door, 'No children. No dogs'. Not even his own grandson, Jacob was allowed to step beyond the threshold.

It was a well known fact that Simon did not like Jacob and resented his presence. To Simon's shame, Gemma, his daughter, got herself pregnant out of wedlock and if that was not bad enough, she proudly let everyone know that she had no idea who the father was. Gemma had a list of possibilities but could not strictly narrow them down to get to the answer. Worse still, half way through her pregnancy, she fell in love with her new beau who made it clear that he did not like children and had no desire to have his own let alone someone else's. Therefore, he gave her an ultimatum that once it was born, she would have to choose between him or the baby. Once Gemma gave birth to her son, she willingly and without any hesitation abandoned him to begin her new life with her boyfriend far from the village. Before Gemma left, she dumped the baby on her father's doorstep. Simon was left with no other option but to keep him. Every time Simon looked at the boy, it reminded him of his contemptible daughter.

James always felt sorry for Jacob. Whenever he went to the pub for a drink, he would watch the boy playing on his own, usually on the swing. When it began to get dark, Jacob would hop off the seat and come running towards the window, pressing his face against the glass, peering inside the pub to take a look at his grandfather who was either pulling pints or laughing raucously with the customers. After a few moments he would walk out of the gate and stroll sadly down the road with his head bowed down. James found it difficult to believe at the time how a little boy, who was deserted by his mother could also be rejected by his grandfather. James thought that Simon's natural instinct should have been to love Jacob all the more and try to make him feel secure. That is what he would have done under those tragic circumstances.

'I don't think this is the right time for pleasantries,' Jacob muttered. 'I just don't want any trouble.' With this, he turned away from James and moved down the bar to serve another customer.

James took his pint and moved towards the corner table and sat in the chair that faced the front door so that he could see his daughter the moment she walked in. Thoughtfully, he wondered if he would instantly recognise her. Would she look like her mother or take after him? He would be happy either way but felt she would be so much prettier if she took after Anna.

James sipped his bitter slowly and listened to the boys in the back room playing pool. He could hear the clack of the balls as they collided and one of the players spitting out profanities whilst the others laughed and mocked his shot. Obviously, they were not very good at the game and were just mucking about. Sighing, James thought to himself that it was a blessing to hear some people having fun. The lighter atmosphere next door was a welcomed distraction from the stifling mood of the lounge.

It was not for the first time that he looked at his watch, since entering the pub. It was now 6:47 pm. Time was passing at a sadistically slow pace. James could feel his stomach knotting with nerves and was afraid that the gurgling noise was loud enough to be heard. That would not be a good thing to have to deal with when meeting Eloise for the first time.

He took another sip of his drink and a movement by the door captured his attention. He just caught it over the rim of his glass. Immediately, he lifted his head and sat up straight, hoping that Eloise had turned up early. However, it was a young man that had walked in. He swaggered into the centre of the room and looked left and right, nodding to certain individuals as he spotted them. The man's eyes settled on James and narrowed to slits. He took one hand out of his pocket and pointed at James. The gesture was sharp and angry and James felt instantly intimidated.

'You!' The voice was deep and hoarse from years of smoking. 'It is you, isn't it?'

'We don't want trouble Jeremy. Not today.' Jacob stepped in.

Jeremy swung around to face the bartender and replied, 'He is the one who causes trouble. He killed Bradley and Adam.'

As his words echoed around the room, the whole place fell into an even deeper silence. Jeremy captured the attention of every ear in the bar.

James was stunned and could only stare at Jeremy in silence.

'You know Adam committed suicide,' Jacob spoke gently. A tinge of sorrow was evident in his tone.

'He made him commit suicide. Adam felt guilty for losing Bradley that day when this bastard took the little lad's life. He could never get over it.' Jeremy was warming up for a fight.

An elderly man, well known in the village as Arthur, stood up and walked towards Jeremy. 'Where did you get an idea like that in your head?'

'I overheard John tell Tom and Ashley Davis. He showed them a scrapbook that Adam kept. It was full of articles about children who survived after being buried in snow,' Jeremy barked loudly. He was determined to have his say. 'Sounds like the whole rotten business drove him to insanity.'

'If you overheard then it was not for yours or anyone else's ears. Have some respect for the poor family.' Arthur spoke with such authority that Jeremy began to listen. After a brief pause, Jeremy bowed his head and backed down.

'Get this idiot a drink will you?' Arthur continued.

'Hasn't he had enough already? I don't want...' Jacob began.

'Yeah, yeah, you don't want any trouble. This boy won't be any trouble to you or anyone.' Arthur slapped Jeremy on the back rather patronisingly.

Surprisingly, Jeremy even with his foul temper made no protest but quietly murmured, 'Nah, I won't be trouble tonight.' He then glared at James. 'Watch your back mate, I ain't finished with ya.' Then he sauntered to the bar and took the glass of whisky that Arthur held out for him.

Everyone watched as he slung back his head and swallowed all of the liquid in one go. He grimaced as he slammed his glass down and demanded another.

Jacob looked wearily at Jeremy, who was swaying slightly and was now gripping the edge of the bar tightly in order to steady himself.

'I'll pay for both drinks,' Arthur assured Jacob, 'and I will make sure he gets home.'

James started to relax a little as it appeared that the show was over. Everyone returned to their drinks and the silence settled in the room like a mist of dust. He was grateful to the old man for calming things down. He hoped that he could just go back to being invisible and wait for Eloise to arrive.

'I really think you shouldn't be here,' Jacob's voice caused James to flinch. He did not notice him leaving the bar and walk over to him.

'I am meeting my daughter in a moment,' James told him firmly.

'What, Emily?' Jacob was suddenly interested.

'No, Eloise, my youngest,' James replied sharply.

'I would not have believed you if you said it was Emily who was coming to see you. She hates your guts,' Jacob cruelly informed him. 'Eloise is a sweet soul. Don't mess with her head, do you hear me? She's a great girl.'

James felt the comment about Emily cutting a deep wound through his heart. He also realised that Jacob was being a bit over protective towards Eloise. He sincerely hoped that they were not in a relationship. Jacob was at least ten years her senior and although, James was not a snob, he did not want his little girl settling down with a bartender. Like any parent, he wanted so much more for her. It could be argued that Jacob was responsible enough to run the place but he did not own it. He could never provide her with the future that she deserved. Suddenly, in that single moment, he realised that because he loved her so much, his protective paternal instincts came to the fore. However, he also became aware that due to his absence from her life, he did not have any rights over her. 'Are you and Eloise?' he questioned, fearful of the reply.

'No, if only.'

Jacob was about to walk away when James stopped him. 'Jacob? Don't you think it's kind of strange that someone who made a mistake as a young child, so long ago, would torture themselves to such an extent? I mean, we all did things as kids but you just let them go.'

Jacob paused for thought, then answered in a serious tone, 'I guess losing the poor boy led to his death. Besides, you have no right asking such questions. Don't you dare try and put the blame on anyone else but yourself.' Jacob became defensive and recoiled away from James as though he realised that it was not right to engage in conversation with him.

Just at that moment, a beautiful woman tapped Jacob on the shoulder and smiled sweetly at him. 'Could you get me my usual?'

Jacob suddenly smiled awkwardly and his cheeks began to redden. 'Yeah sure, Eloise.' He looked from James to the woman standing by his side and after hesitating for a moment added, 'I'll leave you two, to it then. I'll bring your drink over for you.'

'Thanks Jacob.' Eloise's smile widened. Her mannerism was not flirtatious at all but innocent and friendly. James regarded her proudly. Her hair was long and naturally wavy and her make-up was very subtle. An expensive and pleasant perfume wafted towards him. She wore a dress that was feminine and yet demure. Even though it fitted her figure like a glove, it was far from being inappropriate. James stared at her in wonder; she had become the type of woman that he would have wanted her to be. She looked very similar to her mother.

He indicated for her to sit in the seat next to him and with such joy and thankfulness proclaimed, 'You did turn up.'

Eloise just looked at him for a few seconds. Her smile had become awkward and she seemed to be unsure of what to do next. Instead of taking the seat that James had indicated, she chose the one opposite him. The table formed a much needed barrier between them and it somehow made her feel more secure.

Jacob silently placed a gin and tonic before her and slipped away discreetly. He did not want to be any part of this reunion.

'So, you are my father? I mean that merely in the biological sense.' Eloise cautiously opened the conversation.

James was very aware that he had to tread carefully. She was agitated and guarded her emotions closely. One wrong word could make her decide to leave and any chance of seeing her again could be destroyed.

'I have been wanting to see you since the day I was arrested. You were just a baby then.' James found it difficult not to get emotional. He could feel a lump forming in his throat and tears prick his eyes.

Eloise leaned closer and stared straight into his eyes. 'I want to hear you say that you didn't do it.'

At first, James was taken aback by the request. It was clear that his daughter meant business and did not want to bother with idle chatter.

Returning her gaze, he gently put both of his hands down on the table, but refrained from leaning forward in fear of invading her space. He told her emphatically, 'I promise you that I did not kill Bradley Davis. I am an innocent man and I mean to prove it.'

Eloise continued to stare into his eyes for a moment longer, as if assessing him. Finally, she nodded and sat back in her chair. 'So, why were you convicted? Thirty years is long enough to get a retrial and stuff.'

'I am sure that you know the feelings of this village and in fact, the whole of England. They had their man and nothing was going to change that. The police found my scarf wrapped around that flipping snowman. They found a couple of hairs and tested for DNA. I was spotted by a local as I was walking alone in that area. You know how it is here. I am not considered to be a real villager and neither is your mum. We moved here when we got married. So, I was taken in. Of course the DNA was a match but I never even saw the boy or any of the other children. All I knew was that I lost my scarf during a leisurely walk on a crisp, December morning and that meant I was capable of murder.'

Eloise listened intently.

'Very quickly, I was sent to prison and remained there until now.' James bent his head sadly. 'I wanted to see you, all of you but your mum didn't let you. She believed and still does, that I am guilty.'

'That was the belief that I was brought up with.' Eloise was thoughtful. She pressed her lips together until they thinned out into a straight, white line. Her brow was furrowed and her expression held just a hint of pity.

James saw all of this and it gave him a little hope. 'What do you personally believe?'

Eloise shook her head slowly. 'It's too early to say. After all this time, I get to consider your side of the story. It's confusing.' She started to reach out her hand towards James' and then withdrew it quickly. 'You don't strike me as a horrible man. You have kind eyes and a soothing tone in your voice. Besides, I don't believe my mum could make such a huge mistake about a person. She would never have married a murderer.' A nervous laugh escaped her and then she grew serious once more.

'We did love each other once,' James whispered.

'And you still do,' Eloise added sorrowfully. 'I should go. I need time to think.'

As Eloise got up, James asked, 'Will you see me again? Whenever you might feel it is the right time of course.'

Eloise looked down at him and gazed at his pleading expression. Seeing a man look so pathetic and desperate made her feel uncomfortable. 'Yes, soon. I will call you.'

James' voice caught in his throat and he found it difficult to speak. All he managed to say was a weak, 'Thank you.'

He watched Eloise leave through the front door. She did not turn around once which left him feeling disappointed. When she disappeared, he wiped his forehead and found that it was hot and sticky. He felt emotionally drained and completely exhausted. He surveyed the room and found that only Jeremy was staring at him. He quickly glugged down the rest of his drink because he wanted to get out of the pub as soon as he could. James did not like the look in Jeremy's eyes; they were cold and full of hatred. He knew that he would have to be careful whenever Jeremy was around because he was out for his blood. James decided that it would be safer if he made his exit through the front door in full view of the people in the pub.

There was one horrifying thought that scared him. If Jeremy decided to harm him, would anyone bother to come to his aid? Even worse still, would anyone care?

CHAPTER TEN

Just a few early shoppers dawdled up and down the aisles on Saturday morning. James watched them as they clung onto the trolleys and shuffled aimlessly, only stopping now and again to consider whether to buy an item or not. Some merely glanced over the shelves as they moved along, their faces void of any enthusiasm or interest. Most of the trolleys were empty and at first, it was a point of amusement for James. He could never understand why people would bother to get up so early if they could not concentrate on the task at hand. However, with continual observation, he began to conjecture that these people, most likely, had nothing better to do with their time. Perhaps it was because they were lonely and for some strange reason the weekends seemed to be the most difficult to get through for them. Possibly because families are normally enjoying their time together on Saturday and Sunday, while solitary people can only watch and feel even more desolate. Shopping was a way of getting them out of the house, in the hope that they would bump into someone that they knew and have a chat. If they were really lucky they might meet a person who would be willing to spend a little time in the supermarket café and stay to have a cup of tea or coffee. The only thing that James was unable to grasp was why these lonely people failed to get together and make friends with one another. Life would seem so much sweeter but obviously the solution to the problem was not that simple. If it was, then loneliness would be wiped out from earth and people would stop fearing its sting. James quickly realised that he had drifted into solving one of the enigmas of life and that was not what he was paid to do.

James slowly began preparing his own counter. He was usually much more diligent but he could not focus properly on his work that day. Luckily for him, there was no need to hurry because the serious shoppers usually arrived at about ten-thirty. This would give him plenty of time to arrange his delicatessen counter for a visually pleasing effect. Besides, the store was not run like clockwork. The manager was lazy and most of the time stayed in his office, neglecting to keep his staff under control. This resulted with the employees taking advantage of the complacent attitude of the manager by arriving late and neglecting to provide good customer relations. More often than not they were rude and unhelpful because they knew that they would get away with it. Even when the public complained about the service to the manager, he failed to do anything about it and the bad attitude from the staff became the norm. The people could have revolted and done their shopping elsewhere but it was the nearest large supermarket in the surrounding area and the most convenient for them all. Bad practise of the business simply carried on.

Under normal circumstances, James on the other hand, thrived on the boss' ineptitude. He felt like he owned the delicatessen counter and took pride in both his appearance and the food he handled. Health and safety rules became as important to him as the Ten Commandments and his counter was a work of art. Many of his customers commented on how beautifully he arranged the various delicacies that caught their eye and enticed them into purchasing more than they needed or in fact wanted.

Today, his mind was filled with the conversation that he had with Eloise. It was only last night that he had met her and yet every word she spoke and expression on her face was still fresh in his mind. The fact that she promised to see him again was the only thing that he could think about. James felt optimistic that she would believe in his innocence and perhaps use her influence on Emily and Jack in his favour and create a chance of allowing him to win back the love of all his children. He slept soundly that night because Eloise gave him some hope for the future. When he woke up in the cold light of day, he no longer felt so confident about the brighter times waiting for him on the horizon. As he opened the frayed curtain and looked around the room, James realised the reality of his situation. He was still trapped in a nightmare where he was no longer considered to be human, but a detestable, ugly ogre. How could he possibly prove to his children that he did not kill Bradley? James knew that he needed to obtain concrete evidence but where and how could he find it? It all seemed hopeless as without it, he would remain a condemned man for the rest of his life.

'Hello! Are we somewhere nice?' a woman's voice asked amusedly.

James was jolted out of his deep thoughts and quickly looked up to see Stacey Davis standing before him. He had not expected to see her so soon and even though her presence took him by surprise, he was genuinely happy to see her. It was true that he was partly interested in her because of Bradley Davis, but he also found her intriguing. She was sweet and mild mannered, yet it baffled him that she appeared not to recognise him. His face was shown on the television during news time and every newspaper when he first left prison. Surely she would have said something about it, just like his landlord when he first met him. However, here she was, friendly and with a face that could light any room up because of her infectious smile.

'I'm sorry, I was miles away.' James returned the smile. 'What can I do for you today?'

Stacey looked down at the selection of food but it was clear that she had not come to the supermarket just to buy some extra shopping. She seemed distracted and desperately in need of a good listener. James decided that he would give her a gentle nudge in the right direction to open up to him. It was fortunate that he could give her all of his attention that day as there were no other customers to serve. Besides, this was an opportunity that he could not resist taking full advantage of. It could lead to extracting some information that he could use in proving to Stacey and her family that he was innocent. Something was bothering him that was making him feel deeply suspicious about the whole situation with Adam's suicide and his obsession with the scrapbook. It felt wrong and seemed as if it was somehow an admission of guilt on Adam's part. James did not exactly know why he felt like this but it was enough for him to want to find out more about it. It appeared to him that if this lady did have some kind of connection with Bradley's family then perhaps he could wheedle out of her something more about the scrapbook or any kind of information that would help him in his search of solving what really happened on that fateful day.

'Did you see that they are going to close the new school that they just built down the road from here?' James led the conversation with Stacey.

'Are they? No, I didn't know,' Stacey replied absently.

'It has been in the news a lot recently. It was all quite controversial.' James was truly surprised that she was unaware of such an event. 'Apparently illegal materials were used to build it and so the powers that be decided that instead of rectifying the problem, they are going to bulldoze the school down instead. What a waste.'

'I don't watch the news or bother with newspapers. It's always doom and gloom.' Stacey showed her disinterest in the media.

James paused and felt it was the right time to start coaxing her into revealing more about herself. 'Ah, let's change the subject. Hey, did your friend like the platter?'

Stacey lifted her head and looked at James. 'You remembered.' This seemed to please her for some reason. 'Yes she did, it was perfect. Actually, her name is Ashley and she is my husband's sister making her my sister-in-law.'

James' heartbeat quickened its pace. He was sure that the young girl at the time was called Ashley. 'And your husband?'

'Tom. I'm Stacey by the way.' She smiled warmly at James. Talking seemed to lift her spirits. 'Ashley was going to stay with us for only a few days but has now decided to stay longer.'

James could not believe his luck. By total chance, he happened to meet and get friendly with the eldest son's wife who had no inkling who he was. She had managed to miss every news bulletin on the television and every newspaper article about him. To top it all off, she was very eager to talk about her private life. 'That will be nice for you.' He tried not to give away his excessive interest in her family.

Stacey looked thoughtful for a moment and then leaned closer to the counter. 'Not really. Don't get me wrong, it's lovely to see her again but since she returned, Tom has been acting a bit strange. I know that they have not kept in contact since she left Punton and something very serious must have occurred between them to have caused such a rift in their relationship but there is something else and I just can't put my finger on it.' Stacey felt she could trust James and started to give him a full account of her private life and her most inner thoughts on it. 'I feel left out. It is as if they have some kind of secret and are not telling me what it is. All I know is that it happened around the time of Bradley's death. That's their little brother… you may have heard about it. That's now about thirty years ago. He had tragically died after some nutcase buried him in a snowman. Now a friend of theirs has committed suicide.'

James listened intently to her every word. 'With so much going on in Tom's life right now perhaps he just needs time to get his head around it. It's a lot to cope with.'

Stacey stared into James' eyes and he could see that she was giving herself a little time to think about what he had just said. Slowly she shook her head and said, 'May sound paranoid but I don't think that's the problem. There is more to it. Oh listen to me rattle on.' Stacey gave a nervous laugh. 'Telling all this to a complete stranger, no offence.'

'None taken.' James was disappointed that she had stopped talking about her private life. He would have loved to hear more. He was mesmerised by every word that she had just spoken. He was not the only one who had a bad feeling about it all. 'Sometimes it is easier to confide in a stranger than to face those closest to you.'

Nodding, Stacey replied, 'You know what, you are absolutely right.'

Both laughed awkwardly.

'So what happens next? Will you confront them?' James was curious. He knew that he should not push her too hard for more information but could not stop himself from doing so.

Stacey considered this carefully and then replied solemnly, 'I don't think I have got the guts to do that. I will just watch them closely and try to fathom out what is going on.'

'Sounds like a tough position to be in,' James told her truthfully.

'Thanks for listening,' Stacey responded. For a moment it seemed as if she was going to say something but then thought better of it.

James spotted this and asked, 'What is it?'

'It just seems a bit selfish of me. I have been so wrapped up in my own little life that I don't know how you are getting on. I am interested in hearing about you.' She gave a shy but warm smile that indicated a start of a good friendship between them.

'Next time, I'll tell you all about me. Trust me it's nothing interesting,' James grinned as he said this.

'Oh I'm sure there is more to you than meets the eye.' Stacey's smile widened as she was feeling more relaxed in his company now. 'Got to go. So much to do.' She then turned around and walked down one of the isles towards the front of the store. In midway, she turned back and waved to James, who saluted her playfully in return.

As he watched her leave, he murmured to himself, 'If only you knew half of it.'

A few minutes later, James realised that Stacey had not bought anything from the store let alone his counter. Had she deliberately come in just to speak to him? He chuckled to himself for having such a silly thought. It was more likely that the depth of their conversation had caused her to forget what she initially came in for. He reflected over the things that she had said. It was strange that Ashley's return had opened up a can of worms between the two siblings. Did something happen to cause Ashley to leave home in the first place? There were still lots of questions left unanswered that he hoped Stacey would fill the gaps in. The only thing that he could now hope for was that she would find out more and trust him enough to be able to confide in him her knowledge.

CHAPTER ELEVEN

It was the early hours of the morning and Ashley had not slept a wink all night. Her thoughts were constantly pulled towards the funeral and the wretched scrapbook that Adam had kept. It was unbearable to think how much he had suffered over the years with no-one to share his pain or guilt with. Of course, it had never been easy for Ashley either, and there were times when the tragic day played on her mind. In the darkness of the night, she would often wake up in a cold sweat after an excruciatingly painful night of terror. However, she was determined that the one mistake that she had made when she was only a child, would not fester and destroy her life. In fact, Ashley believed that both Tom and her had the strength and will to continue to live carefree and happy lives without dwelling on the past. Tom had managed to build a reasonable life for himself and so had she. Australia had been the best decision that she could have ever made. The distance helped to bury any guilt or shame that she felt. She just wished that her nightmares would cease.

Adam, however, was very different from them. He had always been the sensitive one and it should have been clear to both Tom and her that he was not going to cope with it all. He became withdrawn from the day that Bradley died and that should have been a good indication of his inability to find his own inner strength. Reflecting upon the past, Ashley now realised that instead of being there for their friend and helping him to overcome his bad mental state of mind, they had turned their backs on him. Of course, at the time, it was Adam who chose to end their friendship but they should have at least tried to keep the three of them together. In a sense, she was just as bad as her brother. They were very much to blame for Adam's suicide. Ashley wiped her blurry eyes and sat up. It was all apparent to her now as to what they should have done but there was no turning back the clock to put things right. Perhaps she could do something positive and virtuous to make herself feel less evil but had no idea what that could be.

As the sun crept through the curtains, Ashley gave up on her battle with sleep and decided to open her laptop. At first, her intention was to go through the emails and see if there were any important ones from work. However, her thoughts turned to her mother and she soon found herself typing the name of the independent hospital that specialised in mental health cases, Westcourt House. A picture of the impressive building filled the screen and it brought back memories of the times when she used to walk through the front door and visit her mum. Ashley remembered how much she hated being there. The patients would press their buttons for assistance but the nurses would ignore their cries for help. They would stand in the corridors or by the reception desk and chat amongst themselves. The patients were simply an inconvenience that had to be tolerated. Ashley also recalled that the rooms were generally unkempt and appeared to be rarely cleaned. Her mother's blanket was frequently soiled and the television had weeks of dust settled on the top of it. The furniture was worn and smelt musky. No-one ever questioned the bad conditions that patients had to endure, not even her father, so she grew to accept that all hospitals were the same. When Ashley was a child, she was forced to go there with her father and stay for hours at a time but once she became old enough to go on her own, she kept her visits short, due to the unpleasantness of the place.

After dwelling on the past, Ashley decided to read up on Westcourt House out of sheer curiosity. Opening up one of the sites, she was aghast to see that in the latest inspection, it was deemed inadequate. This meant that the facility would be due to close very soon and her mother would have to be moved to another hospital. This news shocked her as no-one thought to mention it to her. She could not believe that such an important issue did not come up in any of the conversations that she had with Tom and was particularly surprised that Stacey remained silent on the matter as well. Ashley doubted that Tom had spent a moment considering the various options available in selecting the best place to accommodate their mother. Tom no doubt chose to ignore the whole situation as he obviously thought he had more important things to think about other than his own mother. Ashley could not believe just how selfish her brother was. It was clear that nothing else mattered except his own little world. He wallowed in self-pity, focusing only on all the negative issues in his present life. The pressure of his declining job and money were more important to him than looking after his parents. However, it always struck Ashley that Stacey on the other hand, was kind and caring. Surely, at least she would be concerned about this. Ashley knew that there was nothing that she could personally do about sorting the problem because she would be soon returning to Australia. She would have to make Tom face up to his responsibilities in finding and organising somewhere appropriate to put their mother. Ashley was certain that Stacey would be more than willing to help Tom with this.

She turned off her laptop and threw the duvet aside. Ashley then decided to hire a car for the duration of her stay with Tom and Stacey. As soon as it was delivered, she would visit her mother first and then her father. It was the least that she could do. Hiring a car would also give her the freedom of coming and going as she pleased, without having to ask or wait for a lift.

Once the car arrived, Ashley wasted no time to drive to Westcourt House. It did not take long to get there and before Ashley knew it, she was parking the car and staring up at the converted mansion. Even now it gave her the shivers. As she studied the high walls and closed windows, it occurred to her that the last time she had visited her mother was on the very day that she was leaving England. She remembered sitting next to her as she was staring into space and muttering to herself. Not one word had been spoken between them and all Ashley could think about during that long half hour was her packed suitcases and the plane ticket in the top drawer of her cupboard. Her mother noticed the grin on her daughter's face and it somehow made her all the more agitated. It was as though somewhere inside of that shell, her mother still existed, trapped by her condition. She could sense that her little girl was hiding a secret. She rocked back and forth more violently and her weak muttering grew in tempo and in speed until she finally looked at Ashley and whimpered, 'You're going away!'

Ashley was stunned for a moment and seeing the intense hurt and panic on the woman's face, she quickly averted her eyes and mumbled, 'Don't be silly Mum. I'm not going anywhere.'

There was a long pause after that and her mother looked thoughtful. Seeing her expression, Ashley was reminded of the many times that she had given her that same look before she fell ill after Bradley's death. It was a sideways glance, mouth slightly open and those searching eyes, trying to read what was in her mind. She had that look when her P.E. kit went missing when she was seven years old or when some spare change went missing from the jar that lay in the kitchen top drawer just a year later. Ashley could never remember a time when her mother had told her off, only that suspicious and concerned expression on her beautiful face. Even when she denied throwing the old kit into the bin outside her school or stealing the money from the jar, her mother always seemed to know that she was lying.

Suddenly, her mother did something that should have warmed Ashley's heart; she reached out a frail hand and stroked Ashley's cheek. She glowed with the love only a mother could bear for her child and gently whispered, 'I will always love you my girl, wherever you are.'

Instead of reaching out to hold and comfort her mother, Ashley could only think about one thing; the hands on the clock had reached that time for her to slip away in order to catch the plane. There was nothing on this earth that was going to stop her from leaving. So, she pushed her mother's hand away from her face and without another word got up and left. As she walked down the long corridor, she did not even once glance back or hesitate for one moment to consider if she should stay.

Now, here she was again, her hands placed over the steering wheel and staring at the old building. Ashley realised that since living in Australia, she had barely thought of her mother or her father for that matter. All of those sweet and loving memories that she had of them before that tragic day had been swept away. Ashley was not sure if it was due to the guilt of abandoning them both or just simply because she lacked any feelings towards them. However, as she now thought back to how loving they were to her, a tear managed to spill down her cheek. Perhaps somewhere deep down, there was a heart after all.

Breathing in sharply, Ashley wiped the tear away and got out of the car. She paused and stared at the large building once more. The place looked even more run down than it had done all those years ago. The windows needed cleaning and painting and the garden was left in total disarray. If the outside of the building looked a mess, she dreaded to think what she would find inside.

Ashley made her way to the front door which swung loosely on its hinges and every time the wind blew, it rattled. Even before she opened the door, the same musky smell wafted through it, making her mouth curl in revulsion. With the tips of her fingers, she pulled the door open and slipped inside. There was no receptionist or nurse at the desk and the long corridor was darker and dingier than she remembered. Ashley could hear people moaning and crying which she found very disconcerting. As Ashley carried on walking, there was a thumping noise ahead and as she walked closer towards it, a man came into view, bumping his head against the wall. This horrified Ashley and she wondered what other frightful scene she would witness next. At that moment she would have been quite happy to turn around and run but she moved forward. As Ashley walked towards one of the rooms, she could hear a nurse shouting, 'Why don't you just shut up, or I'll beat that temper out of you.' The venom of the voice formed ice on Ashley's back and she physically stepped back a few feet. With as much courage as she could muster, she pressed forward and walked towards the sound of the voice that was now growling incessantly. 'Eat for God's sake. I haven't got all day.' Ashley was now standing just outside the room and peeped in. To her horror, a nurse was bending over a frail, old woman who was holding her head with one hand and a spoon full of grey slop in the other, while whimpering.

At first Ashley feared that the woman sobbing could be her mother and walked quickly into the room and in a strong, loud voice demanded, 'I am here to see Alice Davis, my mother.'

The nurse looked up and stared at Ashley. For a moment she was speechless and Ashley took this for guilt. 'You didn't think anyone would see how badly you treat the vulnerable people here, did you?'

The nurse stood up straight and with confidence replied, 'No, I am surprised that Alice Davis has a visitor or any living relative for that matter. The only person that I ever saw coming here was her husband and he stopped some years ago.'

The nurse shocked Ashley by her remark. 'When did you start working here?'

'Too long ago if you ask me. About fourteen years,' the nurse replied.

'That's when I went to Australia,' Ashley whispered underneath her breath. 'And you work here every day but saw no other visitors?'

'Never… anyway, carry on up the corridor and turn left. She is in room 308.' With this, the nurse turned her attention back to her victim and continued to treat her cruelly and violently even though Ashley had not yet left the room.

As Ashley went back out into the corridor, she could not believe that Tom or anyone else for that matter, neglected to visit her mother for all those years. However, after a bit of consideration, she felt that at least Tom was ignorant of how badly the hospital treated its patients and the state that it was in. It made her feel better to think that if he had known what was going on, then he would have done something about it and not have allowed their mother to rot under these conditions. After all, what kind of monster would that have made him? Surely, just from what she had just witnessed, the inspectors should have closed it down immediately. Perhaps they did not get to see the whole picture. The nurses would have put on a façade and no-one would take any notice of what a mental patient had to say about the place. Ashley was sure of that.

Slowly, she made her way down the passages and tried to block out the wailing and despair behind each door. This was far worse than a nightmare; she had never been in such a disturbing place as this before.

When Ashley reached room 308, she stopped and took a deep breath to compose herself. She was not sure what she was going to find behind the closed door once she opened it. Surely, her mother would have deteriorated and aged a lot since the last time she saw her, especially after living in this hell hole. Her mother might not remember her at all or even become abusive. She must have waited day after day for her husband, son, or daughter to visit her. Ashley realised that after a short while her mother must have felt abandoned and alone. How could she face her now after all this time? Ashley realised that she had to pull herself together. It was her mum that she came to see and she would always regret it if she did not see it through. Sighing heavily, she was about to knock on the door and thought better of it. Ashley finally found the courage to open the door and enter the room. It was completely silent inside and as Ashley looked around, she could see that it was far worse than she remembered from when she last seen it. The furnishings were now more basic than before. There used to be a double bed in the room but now it has a single with a thin blanket over the top. The cushion has no pillow case, therefore, exposing how it had discoloured and turned yellow with age. Ashley noticed that it was the same old carpet but now threadbare and in need of a good going over with a vacuum cleaner. The curtains looked as if they had seen better days and faded with time. The only thing that had not changed was that the dust still lay thickly on top of the table and skirting board. A large arm chair faced an open window that allowed the chilly air into the room. Ashley felt cold so went to close it. Just as she was about to pull it shut, someone spoke from behind her in a croaky voice, 'No, leave it open.'

Almost jumping out of her own skin, Ashley swung around to find a small, wiry old woman sitting in the armchair. She was looking up at Ashley with an open mouth. Her eyes seemed to be pleading with her. She looked very old and her hair was thin and white but Ashley could just make out the features of her once more youthful mother. She knelt down before her and placing her hands gently onto her shoulders, calmly advised, 'The cold will be the death of you. You must keep warm. I will fetch the blanket and put it over your legs.'

The old woman stared into Ashley's eyes and merely replied, 'Death is welcome. I want to die.'

Not knowing how to respond to this, Ashley took a plastic chair from the other side of the room and sat facing her mother. Placing her hands into hers, she examined her mother more closely and could see how time had withered away her mental and physical strength and knew that the absence of her family in her life had a big effect in speeding up the process. When their father got ill, she and Tom should have been there for her to make sure that she was being treated well in the hospital. At least their father had an excuse but she and her brother had none. There seemed to be no recognition in her eyes and that deeply hurt Ashley. Her mother was seeing a stranger before her and not the daughter she once knew. Suddenly, her mother turned back towards the window and began to chant in a weak voice that faded at the end of each phrase.

Heaven or hell
Where should a mother go?
When her poor baby boy
Was buried in the snow.

A dumbfounded Ashley stared at her mother in disbelief. The words cut through her like a sharp blade. Her mother was still clutching to the memory of her dear beloved son in the abyss of her mind.

Tom was a bad boy
A mother ought to know
Shouldn't have let him take
Poor baby in the snow.

Ashley could feel her heart beat faster and faster. The chant was hauntingly horrifying but she could not help but to listen further.

Ashley was a good one
Sweet and kind
Just a little girl
Without her own mind.

Her mother stopped and burst out crying. Ashley was so stunned by what she had just heard that she found herself unable to do anything. She just stood there and watched while her mother tormented herself. Her mother began to rock her body back and forth in the chair and beating her fist at the side of her head. Ashley on the other hand, could not recover from the shock that her mother suspected that her own children were more involved in Bradley's death than what everyone was led to believe. Ashley knew that her mother's mind was very muddled and she could no longer think clearly but the accusation froze her to the core. It accused Tom of foul play and her for doing nothing about it.

'Mum, you don't know what you are saying,' Ashley spat bitterly.

Her mother stopped crying instantly and looked up at Ashley once more. 'Do you have your own mind now Ashley or does Tom still control you?'

Ashley felt as if she was suffocating and sweat poured down the back of her neck even though the room was freezing. For a moment, she just stood still and stared down at the woman before her. Then, with a burst of energy, she ran out of the room and continued to move speedily until she got to the car. She unlocked it, jumped into her seat and started to scream. All of her emotions tumbled out at the same time. She screamed until she felt that she would burst and then sobbed and sobbed. It was an hour before she gained control of herself but still continued to sit in the car for a little longer. Instead of driving to visit her father next as she planned, Ashley decided to make her way back to Tom's house.

CHAPTER TWELVE

Ashley parked her car on the drive and switched off the engine. She did not open the door to get out but remained seated, staring at the front door. Her mind was at breaking point with the chant still whirling around in her head. Ashley's face was flushed and her head was throbbing, making her feel quite nauseous. She was left much shaken after the whole episode with her mother. Her hands shook uncontrollably as she let go of the steering wheel. She held them up to her face and wanted to burst into tears again. When her head began to spin, she opened the door to get some fresh air. The icy wind swept into the car and she sat back in the seat and closed her eyes.

Ashley's intention that morning was to first visit her mother and then her father but now her second objective would have to wait because she needed time to overcome the emotional shock of her mother's revelation. Ashley felt that the best place for her to do that would be to come back here. Even though her eyes felt swollen, she opened them and returned her gaze to the house. On top of everything else, she knew that she no longer belonged in Punton because there was nothing left for her to stay for. Her father had left everything to Tom and obviously lost his feelings towards her. Their mother was unhinged and there was no likelihood that she would ever get better. Ashley never lost her aversion towards her brother but on the contrary it increased after meeting him again. All this made her feel empty, lost and extremely sad. After running away to live in Australia to escape from the pressures of life and living with guilt, Ashley always thought that if one day she decided to return, there would always be a home to come back to. This always brought her comfort and a peace of mind. Ashley now realised that she could never make Punton her home again. The day the bird had flown away it had lost its nest for good.

Ashley's thoughts kept going back to her mother, pointing the finger at Tom and her for Bradley's death. For how long had she harboured her suspicions? Were these doubts, the very cause that ate her away, not allowing her to heal and to return back to her family ever again? Ashley found it difficult to accept that not only Tom but she could be the ultimate reason for her mother's suffering. No wonder the doctors could not cure her, when she silently bore this heavy load on her own head. Perhaps her father came to the same conclusion but daren't speak of it. Just how many people did that one tragic day affect? Did she have any strength left to find out more? It was enough for her to know that her loved ones were completely destroyed because of it. Part of her was itching to run away again back to Australia and leave all this behind her. Ashley knew that from now on Australia would be her true home and once she left, there would be no way that she could ever return to Punton again. The thought of catching the plane once she finished her business here, was the only thing that kept her from losing her mind.

Now, that Ashley's headache was gone, the next thing that she needed to do was to see her father to find out if he also suspected Tom and her of being guilty for Bradley's death. It was time to stop running away and confront what had happened in the past and perhaps then she could bring some kind of solace into her life. She should have done this years ago. Ashley switched the engine back on and headed towards her father's nursing home. It would be a long journey but it was one that she had to make.

Her father had been placed in a charming nursing home that was quite expensive. As Ashley entered the foyer, she was pleased to find the atmosphere was extremely pleasant. A very young and sweet looking nurse greeted her at the front desk with a warm welcome. She smiled gently and with a softly spoken voice asked, 'Is there anything that I can help you with?'

Ashley felt more relaxed and replied, 'Yes, I have come to see my dad. It's Michael Davis.'

The nurse at first gave a surprised expression that changed into a grin and then spoke excitedly saying, 'Oh how wonderful. Mr Davis has not had a visitor for all the time that I have worked here. The nurses that have been here far longer than me said that they had never seen any either.'

This did not surprise Ashley at all. 'I have just come back from Australia for a short stay.' She was not sure why she felt she had to justify herself to the nurse but once she started, the words tumbled out. 'I moved there straight after University and I teach in a secondary school in Melbourne.'

'I understand completely.' The nurse smiled and seeing Ashley's awkwardness changed the subject. 'Your father is a lovely man. I am his main carer and he makes my job so easy. He never complains about anything.'

'That sounds just like him. I can't ever remember a time when he moaned about something.' Ashley followed the nurse as she started to make her way down the corridor.

As they walked, the nurse pointed out the different social areas and explained what went on during the day. 'We encourage our residents to socialise as much as possible. We don't like to see anyone being left behind. That is when the misery and bitterness sets in. We are well aware that a lot of them wished to remain in their own homes but for one reason or another were placed here by their own family. It is a pity that so many children prefer to put their parents into a care home even before they become too much of a burden. But that is the way of the world these days. Everyone has their own lives to lead and we are only happy to have them here.'

Ashley detected a tone of sarcasm in the nurse's voice.

'All they really want is to feel wanted, secure and respected. That's what we try to achieve. They are very often frightened and reluctant to make this place into their new home but we reassure them and they quickly adapt to their new surroundings. They need to keep their independence and have the wisdom to choose what they want to do. The more energetic and green fingered like to help by doing a bit of gardening. We feel that it does them a lot of good. There are no set timetables or too many rules except breakfast, lunch and dinner are served at set times. As long as they are happy and comfortable, then we know that we are doing our job properly. We do make it our duty to know where they are and if they are safe.'

'Sounds like a dream.' Ashley was stunned by how well the place was run. Looking around her, she could see that their whole ethos worked incredibly well.

What struck Ashley the most was how clean and bright everything was. Each room was beautifully decorated and everyone looked content. She could hear enthusiastic conversations and loud bursts of laughter. When she poked her head into one of the social areas, the residents were busy chatting to each other. Some sat around a circular table, playing cards. There seemed to be nurses present in all the rooms and were either plumping up pillows or joining in with the residents. The relationship between all of them was a joy to watch.

'During the summer your dad likes to sit out in the garden. When it gets too cold he stays in the conservatory. It is not to admire the garden but he enjoys the peace and quiet. He reads practically all day. It's his way of keeping his brain active, he tells me.' The nurse giggled and pointed to a patio door that opened out onto a huge conservatory. Even from this distance, Ashley could see that it was well maintained and as she approached the open doors, it impressed her to see that it was filled with various sweet scented flowers. It was as if the garden continued into the room.

Ashley stopped walking and gently placed her hand on the nurse's arm. The nurse looked at Ashley and frowned. 'What is it?'

'You talk about my dad as if he is sound of mind and healthy. I was led to believe that he had deteriorated since I left.' Ashley paused, thinking of the best way to explain to the nurse what she was trying to say. 'When we were kids, Dad became vacant and distant after Mum had a breakdown. He could not cope without her. He left his job and hardly spoke to us or anyone. He was unfit to bring his children up.'

'Perhaps that is something the both of you should talk about today. All I know is that he lives a quiet life and is very rational. There is nothing wrong with his brain.' The nurse gently pulled away from Ashley's grip. 'You will find him in there. Please have some tea or coffee whenever you like.' She smiled and then made her way back to the reception desk.

Ashley replied, 'Thank you.'

The nurse looked over her shoulder and said, 'Your welcome.'

Ashley walked through the wide doors and saw her father sitting in a padded cane chair. A thick book rested on his lap and he sat comfortably with his head slightly tilted. One hand held the book whilst the other dangled over the side of the chair. All of his concentration was directed on reading and it looked as if nothing else could steal his attention. He was smartly dressed and his skin had a healthy glow. His hair was silver but receding from the top of his head. He reminded Ashley of Sean Connery who looked just as handsome and charming in his older age. Any young man would be very happy to look like that.

'Dad?' she said quietly.

Her father slowly lifted his head and stared at her. For a moment he looked puzzled as if he was seeing an apparition. Then he closed the book and letting it drop to the floor, raised himself out of the chair and walked towards her. He smiled and held out his arms to her and asked, 'Ashley, is it really you?'

Ashley put her arms around him and was amazed by how strong he felt. They hugged tightly for a few moments and then her father broke away. He held her at arm's length and gazed at her admiringly. 'What a beautiful lady you have become. My goodness.'

'You look great yourself Dad,' Ashley replied with all sincerity. She let him lead her to a small table that had two chairs at opposite ends. After they sat down neither of them spoke. There was so much that they both wanted to say but did not know where to start.

'I thought you would be…' Ashley searched for the right word, '…vulnerable.'

'Believe me I am; here.' Michael pointed to his heart. 'When you told me that you were leaving, I looked deep into your eyes. I did not see remorse, doubt, love. You were so happy to be leaving that I realised how little you thought of me. You didn't even say goodbye. It was the best wake-up call that I could ever have.' Michael choked back the tears as he was saying this.

'Dad, I didn't mean for it …' Ashley was stopped as her father spoke abruptly.

'You were right to feel that way about me. I deserved it. I shouldn't have let my despair engulf me. I should have thought about you and Tom. Just when you needed me the most I wasn't there for you.'

'I don't blame you Dad. You lost a child and your wife, all at the same time.' Ashley leaned forward and gazed upon her dad. Her expression suggested pity instead of love. From the very depths of her soul, she bitterly agreed with every word that he said.

'I had you two to think about and that should have taken precedence over everything else. I let you down.' Michael bowed his head in shame.

'There are things that I don't understand.' Ashley needed to get some answers and explanations from him.

Her father lifted his head and nodded, indicating that he was listening.

'Why did you agree to come here? You gave everything to Tom. You left nothing for me and stopped visiting Mum. Why is Tom so bloody important? I could have handled it better if you had dementia or something. In fact, I wish you did. But seeing you so normal and happy…' Ashley threw the questions at him all at the same time before he could get the chance to answer the first. Anger and frustration bubbled inside of her. Ashley could feel the blood pump furiously through her veins.

'It's complicated and anyway it's not all about Tom. Ashley, I love both of you exactly the same. I have no favourites.' Michael tried to explain. 'You chose to start a new life and froze us out. Even though you gave me your telephone number, the message was very clear. You wanted nothing more to do with us and so I respected your wishes. As I said before, I couldn't blame you for how you felt.'

'Don't you dare make this my fault,' Ashley hissed vehemently.

'I am not trying to. Tom was struggling financially. Some of it was his own fault, I will grant you. Instead of keeping some money saved back, just in case, he spent the lot. Of course, when his wage decreased, his bills increased. He couldn't stop living the way he had grown accustomed to. It got so bad that he had no choice but to sell his house and move back in with me. It was then that I understood how desperate he must have been. He hid it well but I knew full well he hated every minute having to live under my roof.' Michael continued as Ashley listened. 'I wanted more than anything to make it up to you and Tom. You were on the other side of the planet and as far as I knew, doing well. Tom was here and in need. So, yes I agreed to hand everything over to him. I agreed to everything that he wanted.'

'Did it make you feel better?' Ashley mumbled.

'No. To be honest, no it didn't. But at least I tried.' Michael fell into the seat.

'How could you give up on Mum?' Ashley asked in desperation.

Michael thought carefully about this question as it was not an easy one to answer. 'I went to see your mum for two hours every day for fourteen years. I never missed even one day. Although she was a patient and had carers, I made it my duty to bath and feed her. I loved her more than my own life. However, seeing her slip further away from me with each passing day was intolerable. At first, she would forget my name, then she forgot many of the wonderful memories that we shared. It was as if her illness was corroding the woman that I knew. She locked herself up in her own world so securely, that I could not break through to get inside of it. She was no longer my wife. At times I just wished that she would die and it would all be over. Of course, I hated myself for feeling that way. During the last few visits, she became flustered and distressed when I came within a few feet of her. She would bang her head with her fist and throw anything she could grab at me. I thought long and hard about the best course of action, I really did. Then it suddenly struck me to let go and walk away from her life and never to see her again. Your mother was dead to me.'

Ashley found it impossible to process what her father was saying. It all seemed completely insane. 'I have just come from seeing Mum and she is still aware of everything. At first, I thought she didn't recognise me but she knew who I was. Her soul and consciousness has not gone away, she is still my mum, your wife and very much alive.'

'It must have been one of her good days,' said Michael mournfully.

'I doubt any day is a good day for her. Do you know what? You talk about finally realising that you let me and Tom down? Well, you have let Mum down too. Are you aware of the state the place is in? It's disgusting. They are going to shut it down and Mum has to be moved and no-one seems to give a damn, not even you.' Ashley by now was fuming.

A nurse popped her head in to see what all the commotion was about. Her father gestured that all was fine and so she went away. 'If it has got that bad then it is best that she is moved.'

'Is that all you have to say? Have you seriously gone mad?' Ashley shouted. 'Has the whole world gone mad?'

'Ashley please. We all have to come to terms with the fact that things will never be as they were,' Michael pleaded. 'Too much has happened.'

Ashley stared at her father and all she could feel was great disappointment and disgust. There was nothing more to say and so she immediately got up and said, 'I've had enough. Bye Dad.' With bitterness, she made her way back to the car.

CHAPTER THIRTEEN

When Ashley returned back to Tom's house after seeing her father, she was still shook up by the whole ordeal, feeling angry and disillusioned. The words, 'Your mother was dead to me' kept going round in her mind. How could he have said that? He loved her once; how could that have changed to total indifference? It was as if she no longer mattered or even existed. Ashley was also feeling perplexed by her father's attitude when she questioned him about giving Tom half of the inheritance. He showed no regrets or shame but on the contrary tried to put the blame on her. He felt exonerated from his neglect towards both of his children by leaving everything to one at the expense of the other. How cruel and nasty was that?

Ashley wanted to confront her brother and ask him why he did not tell her the truth about the health of their father and why he had not visited or checked on their mother to make sure that she was properly looked after at the hospital. Tom neglected his duties towards their parents. She was still positive that he had something to do with their father giving him all the inheritance. Tom wanted it and made sure that he got it all. Ashley wanted to tackle her brother about all this but knew that she would have to wait until the next day. Tom would be at the office until late and would want to have a shower when he gets home and go straight to bed. He would not be in any mood for a confrontation and Ashley was not sure if she was ready to face him just yet.

The one person that Ashley wanted to speak to was Stacey. She knew that Stacey was not fully to blame from withholding information from her because she was only doing what Tom told her to do. Stacey was totally loyal to Tom and would have completely trusted his judgement to keep silent. Nevertheless, Ashley felt hurt because Stacey had once been her best and most trusted friend and she should have prepared her for the shock.

Ashley got out of the car slowly to delay going into the house. She hated the thought of confronting Stacey as it was not something that she would enjoy doing but necessary no matter how unpleasant it would be.

As soon as she opened the front door, she could hear Stacey vacuuming one of the rooms upstairs. She shouted up to her but her voice was drowned by the loud noise of the vacuum cleaner. Without taking her coat off, she ran straight up the stairs. Once up there she could see Stacey busily cleaning the carpet. Ashley cupped her mouth with her hands and took a deep breath; she was about to shout again to get Stacey's attention but changed her mind. Seeing the plug near her, she yanked it out of the socket and the noise stopped almost instantly. Stacey had a look of surprise on her face when she turned around to see what had happened.

'Oh, you're back. Did you do anything nice?' Stacey smiled warmly, unaware of what Ashley had discovered.

'Oh, absolutely fantastic. I visited Mum and then went to see Dad.' Her tone was thick with sarcasm. Ashley was struggling to contain her enmity and could feel herself wanting to let it all out in one long scream. Fighting with all her might, she kept her mouth shut for a few moments.

Stacey could see that her sister-in-law was agitated by the tone of her voice and in the way she was standing, with her arms by her sides and fists clenched tightly. She decided that it might be best if she waited until Ashley spoke first.

'Amazing how neither you nor Tom told me about my mum's vile living conditions and that the hospital is on the brink of being closed down. Then again, how would you know when you didn't bother to visit or check on her from time to time?' Ashley was shaking from anger and her voice was full of vehemence.

Stacey shrunk back and began batting her eyelids from tension. Her mouth fell open but she still remained silent.

'Have you or Tom any idea how much heartache and distress you must have caused Mum? Obviously not. She must have been waiting and waiting day after day for you to come until she realised that you abandoned her. Mum must have felt alone and frightened. It makes my blood boil just thinking about it. Both of you are heartless and deserve each other. Both of you make me feel sick. You do realise that an alternative place will have to be found for her. Of course not, why would you?'

Stacey wanted to say something but was too petrified of Ashley to let out a sound and did not want to say anything that could provoke her in any way.

'And my father?' Ashley gave a nervous giggle that seemed to border on insanity. 'He looks pretty healthy to me. He doesn't look, now let me remember your words correctly, "…unable to take care of himself and it became difficult for us to look after him". You stared right into my eyes when you told me that. You lied to my face and didn't have the decency to even avert your eyes from shame or a guilty conscience.'

Stacey could see Ashley's face turning deeper shades of red by the second and she wished for Tom to come back home. Stacey knew that he would be working late so there was no hope of that happening. She would have to stand still and take all the wrath from Ashley on her own.

Then suddenly, Ashley's whole body began to shake and in a fit of rage she bellowed, 'I hate you, I hate you and I hate Tom and everyone! I can't stand this anymore!' She burst out crying and as the tears fell in large droplets and her nose began to drip, Stacey quietly watched and waited until all the tension that was building up inside Ashley spewed out like lava from a volcano and then slowly began easing off and finally died out.

The whole process took more than half an hour and there were times when Stacey thought that Ashley was finally pulling herself together when another bout of tantrums erupted. When Ashley was no longer able to cry and her throat felt red raw, she took a tissue from her pocket and wiped her nose. With red rimmed eyes she looked at Stacey, who was by then sitting on the edge of the bed with the vacuum cleaner lying on the carpet floor.

When Ashley calmed down Stacey began to speak, 'I didn't lie to you, Ashley. I would never do that. It seems that your father deceived Tom and me. That was why he was so eager to leave everything to us. He obviously wanted to be free of the house which was a constant reminder to him of the past and the care home acted as an escape from all his problems. Now he lives a very happy and carefree life in beautiful surroundings and nurses who do everything for him and jump to his every whim, while we struggle to keep up with the payments of keeping him there and without losing all this. The fees are high and are quickly eating away into the money. I'm sorry Ashley but your father is selfish and only thinks about himself. There is something that I need to show you and perhaps then you will find it in your heart to listen to what I might have to say about your mother.'

Ashley merely nodded as she required answers.

Stacey stood up and walked out of the room, expecting Ashley to follow. Once they both got downstairs they went into the lounge. Stacey took a small key from her bag which was by the side of one of the arm chairs. She smiled gently at Ashley and opened a side cupboard, 'Tom never goes in here. This is where I keep all the important letters and things that should be safely stored.'

After looking through a pile of neatly arranged papers, she took a small bundle of leaflets and letters and walked to the table. Sitting in one of the chairs, she started to spread them out for Ashley to see. 'I have already scanned all the various places that we can send your mother. I have thoroughly searched and checked each place to avoid transferring her to that kind of horrific hospital like the present one. I was told by a friend of mine, who had also placed her mother into Westcourt House, how dirty and nasty it had become. She was going to court with proof of the violence that was inflicted on her mother. I decided to go and see the place for myself. Of course, I did not tell the nurses who I was as I wanted to remain incognito. I was horrified by what I had seen, as you now know for yourself after visiting your mum today.'

Whilst Stacey spoke, Ashley looked through the various leaflets and letters of communication between the different homes and her sister-in-law. She wanted to look through them herself before making a decision of whether she approved Stacey's choice or not.

'I didn't tell Tom about this as he has enough problems at work to cope with. Most days he comes home late and goes straight to bed because he is too tired to eat. I worry about him all the time because I really don't know how long he will be able to go on like this. Tom is getting more and more tired and I am sure that his health is suffering. He gets headaches and occasionally pains in his chest and this frightens me. I want to take as much strain away from him as possible. He knows nothing about this and I hope it can stay that way, at least until it has all been sorted out. I want to find the perfect place for your mother and at the same time make the bills less difficult for us to pay.'

Ashley could understand Stacey's reasons in wanting to keep it away from her brother but still wanted to know why she had lied about her dad. 'Okay, I won't tell Tom anything about my visit to Mum. I trust you now that you have shown me the letters and explained everything to me.'

Stacey nodded with relief. 'As for your father, I am so sorry for saying that he is selfish and only thinks about himself. It's just that I felt guilty all this time thinking that I was the reason for him leaving. It's true that I didn't feel comfortable living with him in the same house. I was so used to being with just Tom, that having another person under the same roof was hard. I couldn't relax or do what I wanted. Your father not wanting to look after himself only added to the problem. Anyway, when he moved to the care home I only went to visit him once but he didn't seem to be happy to see me and I thought it was because he blamed me for everything. So when you told me that he was well, it suddenly struck me that he planned it all. That's why it made my blood boil and I said what I said.'

Ashley stared at her and thought back to her own conversation with her dad. It all tied in together. Stacey was telling her the truth and she had to accept it. 'It's okay, I do understand. There is no need to apologise.'

'I was thinking,' said Stacey timidly. She knew that she was stepping on dangerous ground with what she was about to suggest to Ashley. 'Why don't you talk to someone completely unfamiliar to you? I think it could be a good way to release all that pain and anger that is festering inside of you. I think there are other things that are bothering you. Things that you don't want to share with me or anyone else.'

Ashley was stunned by how close to the truth her friend was. She gave a small chuckle, 'Well, I can't see any Good Samaritans around here.'

'What about a priest? We got a new one in the village. Pretty dashing too, if I may say so. He has the most piercing blue eyes.' Stacey tried to lighten up the conversation.

Ashley considered it for a moment. 'I don't know. What good can come out of me pouring out all of my dirty little secrets to a priest? How could it help me to feel any better? It wouldn't have a good affect on him that's for sure.'

'Ooh, what dirty secrets do you have then?' Stacey raised her eyebrows and gave a knowing smile.

'Hey, as if I have. I am not that kind of girl you know.' Ashley smiled and playfully tapped her friend on the arm. Inside, she was thinking how little Stacey really knew about her.

'Shame. It would have made you a more interesting person.' Stacey paused and then widened her eyes excitedly as an idea struck her. 'What you need is retail therapy.'

Ashley stared with astonishment at her friend. 'You are kidding me. I have just had a complete meltdown and you think I want to go shopping?'

'Seriously, a bit of fresh air and something to distract your thoughts is what you need right now. Perhaps some lunch and a drink or two or even three. What do you say?' asked Stacey grinning from cheek to cheek.

'Okay but only because you want to,' Ashley replied. In fact it did seem a good idea to get a change of scenery and maybe have a proper catch up with Stacey. Besides, it couldn't do any harm.

Throughout the journey to town, neither of them spoke. Ashley was looking out of the car window, deep in thought. She could not stop thinking about her parents and what had happened that morning. Stacey on the other hand concentrated on the road as she drove.

Once Stacey parked, they headed towards the town centre and chose a small restaurant that was tucked away in one of the narrow side streets before engaging in some shopping. The tables were covered with white cloth and Ashley was surprised by how extensive the menu was. They both decided to have an 8oz steak with scalloped potatoes and a bottle of crisp, white wine. As they waited for their meals to arrive they drank the wine and talked about the old days when they were growing up together. For the first time in a long time, Ashley felt completely comfortable with remembering and talking about the past because they focused only on the good times that they shared together. At times they laughed so hard that other diners looked at them with puzzled or annoyed expressions. The restaurant was more upmarket and so the customers spoke quietly with one another whilst classical music played softly in the background. Their sudden outbursts seemed out of place and undignified. They both attempted to stifle their hysterics.

'I still can't believe it. You and my brother Tom.' Ashley shook her head and grinned. 'I always thought you were interested in… oh what was his name? The boy who gave you those flowers in class.'

Stacey pretended to choke on the wine that she was sipping. 'Mike Reynolds? The weirdo? Never, that was so embarrassing. Right in front of the whole class. Even Miss Timble giggled.'

'That's it, Weirdo Reynolds. All of the flower heads were missing. He gave you stems.' Ashley had to hold her mouth with her hand to stop herself from laughing again.

'Yeah, it was funny at the time but don't you think we were cruel to him? I mean he did have that crooked leg and funny shaped head. He must have felt so stupid with everyone laughing at him. It must have been awful.' Stacey grew serious. 'Kids can be so evil sometimes without realising the harm they might be causing.'

'So can some adults,' Ashley butted in.

'I know but, when you are young you don't think about it. It's when you look back that you realise what a nasty thing you did. I feel guilty when I think back. If I could go back in time, I would take those flowers graciously and even perhaps kiss him on the cheek.' Stacey gave a subdued smile.

'But you can't so it's best not to think about it.' Ashley was starting to feel uneasy with the subject. 'What happened to him?'

I think it was a year after you left, some kids decided it would be funny to mess around and unfortunately Mike happened to be in the wrong place at the wrong time. You know how sensitive he was and got easily frightened. Even though he was twenty three he acted like a shy five year old. Well, apparently, these kids tied him up and took him to the railway tracks. They had their fun for a while, taunting him until he was so confused and delirious with fear that when they finally untied him, he jumped onto the tracks in the hope of escaping. A train was scheduled at that time and was unable to stop.' Stacey could not carry on with what she was saying and left it hanging in the air, suspended like a black cloud.

Ashley gasped, 'Oh my God. That's terrible.'

'Some people thought that perhaps the kids pushed him onto the tracks but we will never know the truth.' Stacey sadly shrugged her shoulders.

The black cloud was suddenly lifted by the waiter who brought their food to them. He grinned cheerfully and spoke with exaggerated enthusiasm, 'Your steaks. One medium rare and one well done. The vegetables are just coming. Would you be wanting more wine?'

At first both of the women just stared at him and then Stacey replied, 'Not for me. I am driving.'

'Leave the car here and we can get a taxi home. Yes, another bottle of wine please,' Ashley demanded.

'You can have it all. I have to get the car back. Tom would kill me,' Stacey muttered.

Ashley stared at her friend and for a moment paused. 'That's a bit drastic isn't it? Tom would never kill you.'

Stacey frowned. 'It's just a figure of speech Ashley. Come on, the steaks are getting cold.'

Just as they started to tuck into their steaks, the vegetables arrived on a huge platter.

'I won't be eating for a week after this,' Ashley announced.

'And you will have the hangover from hell tomorrow,' Stacey added.

'What, on a bottle and half of wine? It will barely touch the sides,' Ashley chortled. However, she hoped that it would at least numb her mind and stop her mother's song from going round and round inside her head.

'Hey, I have a good idea. After this, I will take you to the supermarket,' said Stacey.

'You certainly know how to entertain someone, don't you?' Ashley replied in mock sarcasm.

'No honestly, they have the most amazing delicatessen counter and the guy who runs it is lovely.'

Ashley raised her eyebrows.

'No, I didn't mean it that way. He is just so easy to talk to, so mild and like an old fashioned gentleman. I would love you to meet him. Besides, the things on his counter are just marvellous. He keeps everything clean and fresh too. You would love it.' Stacey explained eagerly.

'I'm intrigued. Okay, why not,' Ashley responded before devouring her meal.

CHAPTER FOURTEEN

Jeremy was on his fifth pint and was still sober. He was used to consuming large amounts of alcohol and was nowhere near the stage of being even remotely tipsy. He was at that starting point where the strange sensation of fuzziness swam around in his brain and it was a feeling that he enjoyed immensely. He grinned at his four friends as they gathered around a table in the corner of the pub. It was 1:30 in the afternoon and the room was unusually very quiet for that time of day. Jeremy loved it that way, when there was no-one else but his friends to share the bar with or anyone to disturb their private conversation. There were no close relatives of his to frown at the volume of alcohol that he downed or neighbours that rolled their eyes and shook their heads in disapproval every time he swore. Jacob the landlord was far more discreet than his grandfather once was and kept his distance to allow his customers some privacy, only to magically emerge when anyone wanted their glass refilled.

Each of the men around the table either owned or worked in a small family business in the village. This allowed them the privilege of occasionally taking a long lunchtime break and today was one of those days. They began by talking about how their day went so far. Jeremy owned a small local farm and there was not much more to be done that day. He had spent his morning in his small farm shop, serving elderly ladies duck eggs and limp lettuce leaves. Each time one of his customers came in, they would start by saying, 'Ooh chilly out.' Then it would follow by, 'I just can't get enough of these duck eggs, they are so fresh.' When it came to lunchtime, Jeremy thought he would scream if he heard anyone else saying the same thing again. He usually had the patience to put up with the same monotonous chit chat from the locals but today he had enough of it. When the clock struck twelve, Jeremy launched himself out of the chair and fled the farm, almost forgetting to lock up the shop.

There was Joe who worked as a window cleaner with his dad. Together they covered not only Punton but also all of the surrounding villages. They often clashed with other cleaners who claimed they were encroaching on their territory. This never fazed them out because neither Joe nor his dad ever shied away from a fight. They were both robust, violent and enjoyed a good scrap.

Joe was well aware that his father was having an affair with Mrs Bloomsbury down the road. He would never tell his mother about it because this would mean having to betray his father and he would never do that. He always sided with his dad no matter what. He was his hero and someone to admire and follow. Joe knew that his mother was totally oblivious of her husband's philandering ways and he could not see the harm in keeping it that way; what she didn't know couldn't hurt. Joe certainly did not want his parents to split up because he could not see what good that would do. Other than his dad straying now and again, there seemed nothing else wrong with their marriage so why break it.

He knew that his dad would not be returning back to work in the afternoon as he was going to see Mrs Bloomsbury whilst her husband would be slaving away in an office, in London. So Joe decided that he too would skive off work and take the time to spend with his friends.

Andy owned a fleet of buses and one of his successful contracts was to drive children to and from school from Punton and all the surrounding villages. All his close family were employed in the business as well as a few people from the village. Andy also got involved as a driver but was not scheduled that day to collect the children after school. This freed him to join the rest of his friends for an extended break.

When it came to Craig, well no-one was exactly sure what he did. His parents worked as a team in the nearby surgery. His dad was a good and respected doctor and his mother was a charming, caring nurse. He spent his days in the surgery with a broom in his hand or doing other odd jobs until he was told to go home.

Billy was the person in the group who was the constant source of gossip and amusement as he worked in his auntie's hair salon. Most of the younger generation went into the main town for their haircuts whereas the more senior members used the local salon. They were mainly composed of old gossipers that required their hair dyed, rinsed or a perm. There was only one hair style available to them so they all came out of the salon looking more or less the same. There were many occasions when Billy's friends would glare at him through the window and pull faces at him. Of course this irritated the customers and in turn angered his aunt. Most of all, it embarrassed Billy who prided himself as being tough and masculine. Jeremy would always remind him that hairdressing was for girls and effeminate men. Of course, that was not true but that was the way he looked at the job. After his friends stopped laughing, he would quietly remind them that he did not touch anyone's hair but mopped the floor and looked after the equipment. He would then deliberately roll up his right sleeve to show off his ever increasing tattoo collection. He was working on getting a full sleeve and taunted the others that they did not have the guts to have it done.

As they waited for their food to arrive, Billy got up and announced that it was his round and jokingly punched both fists in the air as the rest of the gang cheered and drummed on the table with their hands. A couple of tourists walked through the door and hearing the riot quickly made their way back out and into their car.

When Billy returned to the table with all of the drinks, the subject had turned to James Dickson.

'I can't believe James Dickson came in 'ere and on the day of Adam's funeral,' Joe began.

'He should have stayed under the stone he crawled out of,' Jeremy spat.

'Should've stayed in prison until he rots,' Joe added excitedly. He idolised Jeremy and tried to copy him in every way. For some unknown reason, Jeremy reminded him of his father. It was as if Joe constantly needed his approval which at times irritated Jeremy. At other times, he found it amusing and quite gratifying. Joe would do anything for Jeremy and this could one day come in handy for him, especially if he needed to get out of a tricky situation.

'I think he needs to be taught a lesson,' Billy joined in on the conversation as he passed the drinks round.

The whole table became silent as they gulped down their drinks. Jeremy stared at each one of them over his glass, carefully assessing their mood. The alcohol seemed to be fuelling their dormant rage and caused it to slowly wake up and surface. He could see by the way they sat and fidgeted that they were all brewing for some action. Just a gentle nudge in the right direction would be enough to fire up their appetite for a fight. Jeremy waited for the precise moment to put his plan into action and that was now.

'That bastard deserves a kicking more like,' Jeremy muttered just loud enough so that everyone could hear. He knew that Jacob had better things to do than eavesdrop on their conversation but it never hurt to be cautious.

He had everyone's attention and they all stared at him with their mouths open, almost as if they were in a hypnotic state.

'Have you got a plan?' Craig inquired. His eyes were wide and his grin looked sinister. In his mind's eye he envisaged blood spilling down James' face and he liked it very much.

'Let's put it this way, I know where he works. That's a good start. Last Saturday, I happened to have gone into town and saw him working on the deli counter, for God's sake. He was smiling like he didn't have a care in the world. A kid killer and he is enjoying his life.' Jeremy was doing his upmost to stir things up.

'Well, I'd like to see that,' Craig commented bitterly.

'Why don't we?' Jeremy knew that he was almost there. 'We can drive into town and take a look. Then wait until he locks up for the night. I stayed all day to watch his every move. Would you believe me if I tell you, the boss trusts him to close the whole store by himself? Bloody ridiculous.'

The others groaned with disgust.

'He goes home alone. Well, he won't be going home tonight lads.' Jeremy let that last sentence sink into their minds to germinate and grow into pure evil.

'None of us can drive right now. We have had a fair few,' Andy sounded disappointed.

'And since when has that ever stopped you in the past?' Joe shot back. 'We should use your truck. It's the only vehicle that will fit us all in.'

The rest of the gang agreed in unison, leaving Andy no choice. 'Okay, Okay, I'll drive.'

Jeremy stood up. 'Come on boys let's have some fun.'

'What about our lunch?' Andy moaned.

'Forget lunch kiddo.' Jeremy was in a hurry, he did not want the enthusiasm to dampen in any way. They needed to move now.

Simultaneously, they stormed out of the pub and loaded themselves into Andy's truck. Screeching, he pulled out of the parking space and out onto the road. He just about missed the sign post as the truck meandered from left to right. Getting himself under control, he sped towards town.

Jacob walked out of the kitchen with two heavy, hot plates and stopped in the middle of the room. All of the seats were empty and the dirty glasses on the table were all that remained of the five customers. His face dropped and with a bowed head he returned the food to the kitchen. Jacob knew that it would be a waste of time if he tried to confront them about it. They were aggressive and would have no idea what the words common courtesy meant. All that Jacob could do was to cut his losses and forget about the whole thing if he wanted to avoid any trouble.

CHAPTER FIFTEEN

'I TOLD YOU not to drink all of the wine and I'm glad that I stopped you,' said Stacey whilst grinning at Ashley who was pouting her lips and frowning.

'You didn't give me any choice did you?' Ashley waved an accusing finger in front of Stacey's face. This gesture was not meant as a threat so Stacey just laughed. 'I can't believe you asked the waiter to retrieve the cork,' she continued. Although, Ashley was trying to appear jolly, she still could not shake off that sense of foreboding that was brewing up inside of her. Time was passing quickly and even though she was able to put off confronting her brother until the next day, the inevitable was fast approaching. She was glad that Stacey took the bottle of wine away from her. It had, at first, seemed like a good idea to get drunk and block out the insanity that existed in her life and the stress that she was under, until the alcohol wore off. Yet, she knew that whenever she got drunk, she would say whatever came into her mind, no matter how embarrassing or hurtful it might be. Her emotions were running high and there was a secret that she had kept to herself for many years that would prove destructive, if she was to blurt it out in a drunken stupor. No-one could ever know about it, especially Stacey. Her friend had to remain in complete ignorance because if she ever found out the truth, she would be left with nothing but a broken heart.

Stacey looking pleased with herself said, 'It would have been a shame to waste the wine. We paid enough for it and now it is safely tucked away in my handbag and we can share it back home. Tom is going to be even later home than usual tonight. He said there was going to be an extra meeting, the poor thing.' Her face was full of concern as she hated the fact that the company was taking too much of his time and keeping him away from her. Then, she looked at Ashley and smiled timidly. At least it gave her the opportunity to cheer her friend up and so far it seemed to be working. 'Hey, we could stick on some girly romcom and eat chocolate until we pop.'

'Oh, don't mention to me any more about food. I can't handle another mouthful. Watching a cheesy film sounds good to me, though,' answered Ashley, pretending to be very happy with Stacey's suggestion. She knew that Stacey was doing everything that she possibly could to cheer her up. That was the reason why Ashley did not want to show Stacey how depressed she was feeling. She was carrying a heavy load that was tormenting her inner soul. If she could break loose from the chains of guilt, then she would have the gift of feeling free.

'Come on, we still have to go to the supermarket. I am dying to show you the delicatessen counter and my new friend James.' Stacey pulled at Ashley's arm enthusiastically. Ashley rolled her eyes humorously and let herself be led onto the main town street by Stacey.

The supermarket was only a few steps down the road from the restaurant. Ashley was surprised by how run down it looked from the outside. There did not seem to be any sense of care or pride in the building. She was sure that when she used to come here as a little girl with her mother, the supermarket looked completely different. The walls were white and the large windows sparkled. The tiled floors were washed and polished to such an extent, that she had to be careful not to slip and fall. Once she became more confident and sure of her footing, it became a source of amusement. Ashley constantly begged her mother to allow her to push the trolley so that she could run speedily with it and then lean slightly back, gripping the bar tightly and placing both of her feet flat on the floor. She would then skid across the aisle, nearly knocking over the other shoppers. She soon discovered that the quicker she ran, the further she could slide and she became more and more adventurous with each attempt until one day, she lost control and fell into one of the displays that had been placed in the middle of the aisle. Her trolley smashed into a stack of soup tins, knocking them down like pins in a bowling alley making them roll around the floor in different directions. They were heavy and sharp and several of them landed on her head, the back of her neck and bruised her hands as she struggled to clutch her head for protection. It seemed as though the avalanche of cans were endless and so was the pain inflicted by them. Ashley fell to the floor by the weight of the cans and found herself buried beneath them, struggling for breath. It was then that Ashley started to panic as she could feel her lungs were ready to burst from the lack of air and that death was sure to follow.

Eventually, what seemed to Ashley like a lifetime, her mum pulled her out from under the rubble and she was able to gasp hungrily for breath. She looked up at her mother's worried face and then burst into floods of tears.

Ashley shuddered from reliving that horrible incident.

'What's the matter?' Stacey asked full of concern.

'Oh nothing. Bit grimy though, isn't it.' Ashley grimaced.

'I guess so but I only buy from the one counter. It doesn't fit at all with the rest of the place.' Stacey paused for thought. 'Bit like James, the guy who looks after it really. He doesn't fit in with the place either.' She shrugged her shoulders and pulled Ashley through the sliding doors.

Stacey led the way to the counter which was at the far end of the shop. It was tucked into a corner and Ashley was surprised that anyone could spot that it was there. It was not brightly lit like the rest of the counters and appeared empty.

Stacey stopped and just stared at it. She looked perplexed and murmured, 'Where is he?' She walked right up to the counter and noticed a note taped to the front glass. As she read it, her shoulders slumped, 'The delivery has not arrived and so this counter is closed today.' She turned to Ashley and moaned, 'I was going to let you choose some bits and pieces for tonight.'

'Stacey, it's really okay. I don't think I will want to eat anything until tomorrow to be honest,' she said smiling warmly. 'Come on let's go back home. I'm looking forward to our girly evening.'

Stacey grinned and replied, 'Okay. Maybe another time eh?' and together they walked out of the shop and made their way back to the car.

*

Down in the dingy cellar, James was totally oblivious that his favourite customer had come to visit him. He was not working on the delicatessen counter that day because the deliveries of the goods had not arrived. The boss, instead of sending James home, decided to give him the task of tidying and cleaning the cellar. James was pleased about that because he desperately needed the money. When James descended the steps that led him down into the basement, he was aghast by its neglect and lack of hygiene. The place looked more like a junk yard than a storeroom. Everything was scattered all over the place. It would be difficult to find anything in such a mess.

He could hear squeaking and scratching noises from the darkened corners and see cobwebs hanging down from the ceiling that reached out to stroke his face. James felt incredibly itchy and began to scratch his head, arms and shoulders. There was a lot of work that needed to be done and James was determined to accomplish the chore in his usual meticulous manner. He looked at his watch from time to time and could not believe how the time was passing quickly as it normally does when one is busy.

James was feeling very tired and his muscles ached. He had managed to sweep and clear the floor and had just started to stack the stock into neat piles. His arms hurt when he tried to place the heavy crates of tinned tuna on the top shelf so he decided to focus on replenishing the lower ones. James did not see the point of straining himself on a job that was not part of his responsibility, besides he already managed to make a huge improvement to the place.

His stomach began to growl as he had not eaten since breakfast time. James was tempted to go back into the supermarket and buy something to eat but decided against it because he was feeling grubby. It was not one of the cleanest jobs that he ever had to do. He could not touch even the smallest morsel until he had a long and soothing bath back home.

He worked throughout all of his breaks including lunch time. It was not because he felt compelled to finishing the job but simply because he felt uncomfortable being covered in dust and dirt. There was no way that he could sit and relax in that state. His nose tickled continuously and his throat felt dry and grainy. Suddenly, he got a coughing bout and he found himself unable to stop. He threw down the broom and made his way up the stairs and out of the cellar door that led outside the back end of the store. This part of the building tended to be empty as it was solely used for large lorries and trucks to deliver the weekly stock. He leaned against the wall and closed his eyes. The fresh, cool air felt good as it swept through his hair and caressed his skin. It felt like a gentle massage and helped him to relax for a few moments.

Earlier on, just as Stacey and Ashley left the store, Jeremy and his friends came in. Like the girls but for different reasons, they too were disappointed after seeing the note that James left on the glass and huffed angrily as they stomped out of the store. They lit their cigarettes outside the supermarket, feeling annoyed by missing the opportunity of having a bit of fun on James' account.

While James was standing with his back against the wall, Jeremy decided to have a look around the corner of the supermarket to see what was behind it out of sheer curiosity. To his surprise, he spotted James and for a moment stood motionless, glaring at him with venom in his eyes. He then nodded his head to his gang to come towards him. When the men realised why Jeremy wanted them by his side, they could hardly contain their excitement. They could not believe their luck in finding James alone and in such a deserted area. It was now time for them to settle their long awaited score and there was no-one to stop them. James, with his eyes shut, had no idea that they were creeping up towards him until he felt someone punch him to the ground and then blows pounded heavily over every part of his body. He felt his stomach, head and face rip with unbearable pain as steel toed shoes kicked him again and again. He heard the screams of triumphant joy as blood gushed from his nose, split skull and gashed mouth. His teeth fell onto the concrete ground as the blood spilled from his mouth. James could not cry out for help because he was choking on his own blood or try to take a look at his assailants because his eyes were heavy and swollen. He just lay there taking all the abuse that the vindictive cowards were throwing at him until their voices faded into the distance and darkness fell upon him.

Suddenly someone bellowed out, 'Hey what do you think you are doing!' which made the group scarper, fully satisfied with the damage that they had inflicted on James. As they ran, pumped up with adrenaline, they laughed and shouted in jubilation. It was the best fun that they had for a long time.

The man who chased the gang of men off, tried to get a good look at them but they ran and disappeared far too quickly from his sight. He took off his glasses and wiped them on his shirt. He was shaken by his sudden surge of courage in trying to stop a gang of violent men beating the hell out of their victim. He acted without thinking about the possible consequences of them turning on him. This thought made him feel sick to the stomach and he felt faint. He wiped his sweaty forehead with the back of his hand, and then put his glasses back on.

He stared down at the bloody mess on the floor and was not sure if the person was still alive. He had been kicked in the face with such aggression that it was no longer recognisable and there were no signs that the poor broken being was still breathing. The body lay completely motionless on the ground in a pool of blood and looked as though it had been dipped in crimson paint.

Taking his mobile phone from his pocket, the man began to dial for the emergency services. He leant closer to the person on the floor and recognised the shirt and trousers that he was wearing. Squinting, the man tried to make out the face but it was so badly damaged that it was impossible to do so. Judging by the clothes and being close to the cellar, he realised who the victim was. All that James' boss could say was, 'Oh my god, no!'

CHAPTER SIXTEEN

It was 4:30 pm when Ashley and Stacey finally got back home, and the light had dwindled away behind grey clouds. It was already getting dark but the gloomy weather made it feel more like night time than late afternoon. They giggled like school girls as Stacey opened the front door and switched on the lights. They were both carrying bags full of treats.

On the way home, they had decided to stop off at an off licence to buy another bottle of wine. They both came to the conclusion that they might as well make the most of what had been a lovely afternoon and carry on partying until Tom came home. They chose the one that they drank at the restaurant and were surprised to see that it cost almost half the price. Frivolously, they could not help themselves to also buy bags of crisps, popcorn, chocolate bars and many other bits and pieces just to make it more fun. They assured each other that the selection of goodies would help them to soak up the alcohol.

Ashley was surprised to find that her spirits had been lifted and revelled in the fact that for once, she did not have to think about anything more than just having a little bit of childish fun. For far too long, Ashley had to be responsible for herself and the children that she taught. Not having the time or inclination to get married and start her own family, she put all her energy into each pupil that she taught in her class. At times it was very rewarding but on others, it was soul destroying as she tried to deal with situations that were beyond her control. Straight after leaving University, her path led to a life of independence. She did not have the comfort of her parents' love to shield her from the day to day grind of adult life. Of course, she had no choice but to allow fate to whisk her away to foreign shores. It seemed so strange that she passed her degree so easily and was successful in getting a job immediately. So many other class friends had told her time and time again about failed interviews. She seemed to sail through hers without a problem. Perhaps those decisions that a person carefully ponders over are not entirely of their own choosing. Maybe, there was something else that had already made those decisions for them and pulled them in the direction that they were meant to go in. There were moments when Ashley considered this and quickly brushed it aside. It all seemed too sinister and strange to contemplate.

'These bags are so heavy.' Ashley puffed as she placed her load onto the kitchen table.

Stacey smiled and placed her bags next to Ashley's. She then rummaged around each bag until she found the wine and put it into the fridge. Then, she opened her handbag and took the other bottle out, wiggled it at Ashley while placing it next to the other one.

Ashley watched her intently and could not believe the lengths that Stacey went to in order to cheer her up. She had her own problems to worry about and yet she still put all her efforts to ease the pain and suffering that her friend was going through. With gratitude and warmth in her voice, Ashley said, 'I really appreciate what you did for me today. I just want you to know that.'

Stacey grinned at Ashley and winked. With intensity in her voice she said, 'Oh believe me, I needed this as much as you did.'

Ashley smiled and continued, 'There is only one good thing that has come out from me coming back and that is seeing you. Many years have been wasted from not keeping in touch and allowing our dear friendship to drift into nothingness. I just can't believe how I could have let it happen. I guess when I left, nothing really mattered apart from me wanting to get away from my family. So I let go of everything that was really important to me. It all seems so stupid now.'

Stacey regarded Ashley with pity. She was aware that her friend was carrying a lot of emotional problems but was still uncertain as to the extent. Judging from Ashley's overall behaviour since she returned, Stacey was convinced that there was something seriously troubling her that she was refusing to talk about. This frustrated Stacey because if Ashley could not bring herself to confide in her then how could she help? The only advice that she could keep giving Ashley was to see someone outside of her own circle that she could talk to. 'Have you given any more thought as to whether you would like to talk to our priest?'

Ashley looked thoughtful and said nothing for a few minutes and then finally whispered, 'Perhaps.'

Stacey decided that this could be the perfect time to try and press Ashley into telling her the truth about the estrangement that existed between her and Tom. 'I don't understand why you and Tom have become so distant and dare I say, hateful towards each other.'

Ashley butted in sharply, 'And I hope that you never do.' At the same time, she was thinking to herself that if she did, it would break her dear friend's heart. Ashley hated being sharp with Stacey as she was the last person to deserve it. Then again, she did not warrant all the lies and secrets that were hidden from her.

The harshness in Ashley's tone made Stacey fully aware that she should drop the subject altogether. She was just tapping at a brick wall with no hope of breaking it down. In fact, through her persistence, she was in danger of ruining her relationship with Ashley altogether.

Changing the subject quickly, making sure that she made her voice sound more lively, Stacey remarked, 'Well, we have the evening to ourselves so fancy getting changed into pyjamas and taking our make-up off? You know? Get really comfortable. I have some amazingly soft blankets we can snuggle into as we watch the film.'

Ashley managed a weak smile but seemed to brighten up at the thought. She was relieved that Stacey had dropped the matter so quickly. 'That sounds like a great idea. I can't remember the last time I relaxed in such a way.'

'Glass of wine before we get ready?' Stacey chuckled. 'The one from the restaurant is still chilled. By the time we finish the bottle the next one will be ready too.'

'You are full of the most perfect ideas.' Ashley nodded enthusiastically.

As Stacey reached for two wine glasses from the top cupboard, Ashley took the bottle out from the fridge.

'You don't start work until two weeks time, do you?' Stacey asked.

Ashley nodded her head and asked, 'Why?'

'Well, I don't know when you are planning to go back to Australia but I would like you to stay for as long as possible. That would make me very happy. I love having you here.' Stacey answered coyly.

Ashley felt that Stacey's reason for wanting her to stay longer was not only because she wanted to spend more time with her but she was still hoping that her and Tom would somehow renew their relationship. 'I would love to but I will have to go back in the next few days because I have to give myself enough time to sort things out back home and prepare my lessons for the next school term.' She shrugged her shoulders hoping that this answer would satisfy Stacey.

'Yes but one more week shouldn't make too much of a difference, would it? That still gives you a whole week to prepare for school and do what you need to.'

Ashley did not want to argue with Stacey about it and simply said, 'Okay.'

After gulping down their glass of wine, both of them went to their bedrooms to get ready before settling down in front of the television.

It was not long before they emerged from their rooms and met up in the lounge. Stacey took the rest of the unfinished wine from the kitchen together with the bags containing the goodies and placed them on the table.

Stacey opened a drawer and to Ashley's amazement it was completely full with DVDs.

'How many have you got?' she asked bewildered.

'Lost count, there are more in the drawers over there.' She pointed across the room to a huge chest of drawers. 'Some are Tom's as well.'

She continued to rummage through them. 'I don't know why we bought so many. Tom and I watched most of them just once or twice. We liked the look of the films when they first came out but after watching them a couple of times, we placed them back into the drawer and left them there. The plot and the jokes simply lost their appeal.'

'I guess you grow tired of things and can't bear to go through them all again and again.' Ashley seemed deep in thought.

Stacey looked up and asked, 'We are still talking about DVDs aren't we?'

Ashley glanced at Stacey and smiled. 'Of course we are.'

'Good,' Stacey remarked and carried on choosing a selection of films.

Stacey picked ten films to choose from and placed them in a pile on the coffee table in front of the two seat settee that Ashley was lounging on. She then took a small table from the corner of the room and placed it next to the armchair that was nearest to Ashley. She refilled the glasses with wine and switched the television on.

Turning towards Ashley, Stacey pointed to the pile of DVDs and said, 'You can choose first.'

Ashley's smile dropped as her attention was drawn to what came up on the screen. Stacey was partly covering her view so she cried out, 'Stacey could you move please and turn the volume up.'

Seeing Ashley staring at the screen, she quickly stepped aside and looked at it to see what had caught Ashley's attention. Grimacing, she curtly replied, 'It's just the news. You know I hate watching it.'

Ashley disregarded Stacey's whining and told her to hush. Giving up, Stacey took the remote control and turned the volume up.

The newsreader looked very serious as he leaned forward behind the desk where he was sitting, with his hands clasped together, broadcasting an account of a main headline of the day. 'James Dickson, the man released from jail recently for the murder of Bradley Davis, thirty years ago, has been admitted into hospital due to a brutal attack. The five men who were responsible for the assault on Mr Dickson ran away from the scene when Sam Howes, the chief manager of the supermarket intervened by shouting out and then bravely chased after them. Mr Howes regrets that he did not manage to get a good look at any of the gang members and is therefore unable to identify them.' A photograph of Mr Howes was shown upon the screen and it was difficult to believe that someone of such a small stature with little round glasses that were out of proportion with his huge round head could have succeeded in scaring off the five violent men. The newsreader continued, 'Regretfully, nothing was recorded on the CCTV because it was not working at the time of the crime.'

Stacey was watching the news reluctantly. She hated any form of violence and always shied away from watching it.

Ashley sat still and gaped at the screen.

'James Dickson underwent surgery this afternoon due to his injuries and is said to be in a stable condition.' After the presenter finished his sentence, there was a replay of the scene when James first left prison. Stacey could not see James' face because it was covered with a jacket and was still left in ignorance as of whom they were talking about. It was not until a recent photograph of James popped up in the corner of the screen that she gasped. The photograph had been taken while he was in prison at a charity event which involved some of the inmates.

'It can't be,' Stacey muttered in shock.

Ashley turned and looked at Stacey, who had grown pale and was pointing at the photograph on the screen and said, 'What is it? You know all about him, don't you?'

Stacey shook her head slowly and explained. 'No, I didn't see the news after he left prison. I had no idea what he would look like so many years after Bradley's…'

By Stacey's reaction, a chilling thought crossed Ashley's mind. 'You have not seen him recently, have you?'

Stacey tore her attention away from the screen and murmured, 'James on the deli counter.'

Ashley frowned at first then her expression changed to one of sheer horror. 'You spoke to James and made him your friend?'

Stacey looked as though she was about to burst out crying. 'I didn't know who he was. I would never have gone near him if I knew. And we are not really friends just acquaintances. Someone with whom I had a little polite conversation with while out shopping, that's all.'

'You were very determined for me to meet him earlier.' As Ashley said this, she regretted it. Stacey looked completely lost. Ashley quickly turned the television off and ran to her friend's side. 'Stacey, it's okay. It's not your fault. How were you to know?'

Tears ran down from Stacey's eyes. 'Bradley's killer of all people. I feel like I've let you and Tom down.'

Ashley tried to soothe Stacey who was increasingly becoming more hysterical.

'What kind of judge of character am I? I thought he was a sweet and gentle man. He… he… he killed your little brother in such a horrible way. He's an evil monster.' Stacey's voice intensified in volume.

'Stacey, listen to me. None of this is your fault. You are a good judge of character. Just don't go back to the supermarket and we won't talk about this any more.' Ashley did not like seeing her friend so distressed.

'What about Tom?' Stacey whimpered.

'What about Tom, for God's sake?' Ashley was becoming frustrated.

'We vowed never to keep secrets from each other. How can I face him knowing that I betrayed him and his family? I will never forgive myself. I will have to tell him as soon as he gets home.' Stacey was staring with tears in her eyes straight into Ashley's as she was saying this.

'No, you won't. Think about this carefully. It was a huge shock to you, I can clearly see that but what would be the point of telling Tom about it? You could hurt your marriage. There is no indication as to how Tom would react to your revelation. He has always been unpredictable. A tiny secret won't matter and I'm certain that Tom has one too, everyone has.' She spoke softly and calmly and she was pleased to see that it was helping Stacey to pull herself together.

Stacey gave a slight nod but was not utterly convinced that she should keep it from Tom. 'Might as well put a DVD on then.'

Ashley sighed, 'Another glass of wine should help to calm our nerves.'

Ashley patted her friend's hand and switched the television on again. She was relieved to see that the news was over. Picking up the first DVD from the pile, she placed it into the player and sat back down on the sofa. Stacey watched her do this in silence.

As the film started, they both stared at the screen but neither of them was in the mood to watch it. Stacey was still shaken by her discovery but felt even worse, knowing that she still sympathised with James. He would be in hospital, suffering and in great pain. She could not bear to think as to what would be going through his mind right now. He had served his time and was still being persecuted. Another part of her knew that he murdered a child and destroyed a wonderful, loving family that she was a part of. Stacey felt that he might deserve the wrath of the people but not the beating and hoped that those responsible would be brought to justice. Her mind was in a muddle and she could not come to any conclusion with her reasoning of the situation. Stacey liked James and it was difficult for her to judge him harshly. As a result she could not concentrate on the film but stared blankly at the television.

Ashley too, was lost in her thoughts. It appeared that her nightmare was never going to end. Since that dreadful day, thirty years ago, so many people had been hurt, lives destroyed and the guilt of it all was eating away at her as she remained silent. She quietly gazed across at Stacey and felt sad that she had to stop her from telling Tom about her friendship with James. Ashley could never be sure how her brother would react to even the most trivial things. Sometimes the best policy in life can be to keep silent and say nothing. The problem with this situation is that the sweet, innocent Stacey completely believes in the concept of honesty in marriage and would find it difficult to hold something of such magnitude from Tom. It would always remain on her conscience and she would never be comfortable in looking at Tom in the face again. Secrets and falsehoods from that tragic day, were the very cause of the whole mess that the guilty and innocent found themselves in. The truth might have prevented the torment and suffering for many people who might have found a way through the darkness and into the light and a more hopeful chapter might have resulted for them all. It was at that moment of her reflecting over things that Ashley decided that she would go and see the priest. Perhaps he could offer her some much needed wisdom and guidance to bring an end to all her demons and lay them to rest.

CHAPTER SEVENTEEN

Eloise was at her mother's house when the doorbell rang and when she opened the door, two police officers were standing on the doorstep. Both officers lived in the village so Eloise smiled and greeted them in her usual friendly manner by saying, 'Tony, Maria, what brings you to us today?'

Tony on the other hand responded to her greeting in a formal manner, sending shivers down her spine. Although, he was trying to use a more professional approach, his face showed that he had some distressing news to convey. Eloise then turned her attention to Maria, who had an odd expression. It was almost as if she was not sure how to behave. She was frowning but her eyes were full of pity. She bit her lips nervously but failed to utter a word. Something was definitely wrong and Eloise knew that she would shortly find out what it was.

'Is Anna Wright home?' Tony asked with a firm voice.

'Yes. Of course. Come in.' Eloise replied. She led them into the lounge and gestured for them to sit down. They both remained standing for a moment as they felt very uncomfortable with the situation they were in. When

Eloise left the room to fetch her mother, they glanced at each other and then perched themselves on the edge of the settee. They waited for a few seconds when Eloise and her mother entered the room.

Anna looked at them anxiously as she rubbed her hands with a dish cloth even though they were already dry. She knew that Tony and Maria did not come to exchange pleasantries but were there on a serious matter. Various thoughts went round in her head that confused her to such an extent that she did not know what she was doing. The officers just watched her, allowing her to settle down before breaking the bad news to her.

Tony was the first one to speak. 'Mrs Wright, I have come to inform you that your ex-husband, Mr James Dickson has been taken to casualty after sustaining severe injuries.'

Anna closed her eyes with relief when the word ex-husband was mentioned. She was sure that something must have happened to either Jack or Emily. Opening her eyes, she cut in abruptly, 'And what has that got to do with me? As you said, he is my ex-husband and none of my concern.'

Eloise stared at her mother dumbfounded and murmured, 'Mum, don't be so mean.'

'I am sorry but there was no-one else we could inform. We just thought perhaps you should know and of course the rest of the family.' Tony was feeling awkward by now.

Eloise stepped towards them and responded gently, 'Thank you. I'm glad you came to tell us. How bad is he?'

A gang attacked him whilst he was taking a break from work. He is in surgery for two emergency operations. I am sure the doctors will be able to give you more information,' Tony explained.

'My God,' gasped Anna. Even though she felt hostile towards James and could not forgive him for what he had done all those years ago, no-one deserved to be put through such brutality. Besides, she had loved him once. If she disregarded his anguish and felt nothing towards his present condition, it would make her a cold and heartless woman and she certainly wasn't that.

It was not long before the two officers left and as they walked back to the police car, they felt relieved that this particular task was over. When Eloise saw the car disappear down the road, she picked up her bag and started to make her way to the door. She was devastated by the news and wanted to know exactly how injured her father really was.

Anna was certain that her daughter was going to go straight to the hospital to see her father. Even though James was an evil man, it would not stop Eloise from feeling sorry for him and giving her support. Out of all her children, Eloise was the most gentle and kind hearted. Anna felt that it was not always a good thing in this day and age, wishing that her daughter could be a little more tough and selfish like her brother and sister. People often took advantage of her good nature and being her mother, there was no surprise that she was not going to be happy about that.

'What are you doing?' Anna asked out of concern for her daughter.

'Going to the hospital.' She replied in a voice that slightly trembled.

'I'll drive.' Anna was adamant about her proposition to Eloise.

*

So, here she was at the hospital, listening to the heart monitor blip steadily and watching the rise and fall of the fluorescent green light that was making her feel drowsy. Her mother had just left the room in order to get a breath of fresh air. Even she could no longer bear to look at the state that James was in.

When Eloise first saw James lying there, she was horrified. His face was barely recognisable as the blood seeped through the bandages that were wrapped tightly round his head. The congealed blood formed dark clots that ran down the side of his bruised and swollen face. His lips looked torn and the blood that had trickled out of the side of his mouth now formed a dry river that ended under his chin. His breathing was laboured because of the repeated heavy blows inflicted on his chest. James looked a pitiful sight and Eloise could not help but to wish that she had been a lot nicer to him when she met him at the local pub.

Suddenly, James groaned.

Eloise sat up in the corner chair and gazed over at him.

He moaned again but this time a lot stronger and louder.

Eloise got up and moved towards James' side. She took hold of his hand and stared at him. Her heartbeat quickened as she held her breath in anticipation. The doctor had warned her that the full extent of the damage to his brain would not be known until he woke up. Even though the surgeon felt that the operation was a success, he could not be absolutely sure if James would make a complete recovery.

'It hurts,' James mumbled. His voice was thick and gravelly.

'You're back,' Eloise whispered excitedly and ran out of the room to fetch a nurse or doctor. She ran down the corridor shouting out, 'Nurse? Doctor? He's woken up!'

Eventually, she found a nurse who was walking towards her, frowning, 'What is all the racket about?'

'It's James Dickson. He has woken up.' Eloise informed her breathlessly.

The nurse followed her back into the room where James was now stirring. His eyes were barely open and looked like slits. He appeared to be in a panic.

The nurse bent over him and took his pulse. With a blurry vision, James tried to see her face. He could just make out the nurse's uniform and whimpered, 'Am I paralysed? Can't move.'

'Mr. Dickson, you have had two major operations and heavily sedated. You won't be running around for quite a while. Do try to relax,' she explained while smiling tenderly and then continued speaking but in a more soothing tone, 'you must rest and try not to move. The doctor will be here in a moment to check you over and explain about the medical treatment that has already been given to you. Believe me, you are over the worst now.'

She stood up and turned towards the door. Eloise quickly asked, 'He is alright though, isn't he?'

'Mr Dickson seems to be coherent, which is good news. The doctor will be able to tell you more once he has examined the patient.' The nurse assured Eloise before leaving the room.

Just as the nurse left, Anna returned with two cups of steaming hot coffee. 'Thought you could do with this,' she told Eloise. As she handed the large, polystyrene cup to her daughter, she paused and asked, 'What is it?'

'Dad has woken up and the nurse has gone to get the doctor. What a relief.' Eloise could barely contain her joy.

Anna replied sincerely, 'Yes, what a relief.'

It was not long before the doctor entered the room with his clipboard and pen. His stethoscope dangled carelessly around his neck and his glasses were perched on the end of his nose. He ignored the two women and went straight to James. He studied him carefully for a few moments and then bellowed in a loud, confident voice, 'Under the circumstances, I think that you are extremely lucky.'

Eloise and Anna stared at the doctor with astonishment. How could he possibly say that James was lucky after what he had gone through?

'What happened?' James inquired. His voice was clearer and he appeared less disorientated.

'Where do I start,' the doctor replied and began to flick through the notes on his clipboard. 'You have severely bruised kidneys due to blows to the small of your back but the injury could have been a lot worse. Damage to the intestines caused bleeding and possible blockages which in time would have released bacteria into the bloodstream causing septic shock. Surgery to prevent this from happening was successful otherwise the outcome would have been fatal.' He was in full flow and his enthusiasm for medical science prevented him from showing any empathy towards his patient.

Listening to the extent of the injuries was a lot for James to digest. All he could do was to try and understand everything that the doctor was telling him.

The list continued. 'You have three broken ribs but luckily neither your heart nor lung was punctured. Urgent surgery was required to correct a compound fracture in three places to your right arm. The nerves and blood vessels were unharmed. A fracture to the skull meant bruising to the brain. We will monitor this in order to track progress. Fortunately, there was no bleeding within the brain. Soft tissue around the eyes will heal given time and we suspect no damage has been caused to your eyesight. When the swelling goes down, we will do further tests. The surgery to reposition the bones, in your right cheekbone, into their original configuration was a success. If the fracture was around the eye a more advanced surgery would have been necessary.'

'How long before I can go home?' James asked regardless of what he had just been told.

'The body has been through a lot of trauma but will heal in time. The psychological damage however…' At this point the doctor shrugged his shoulders. 'We are giving you antibiotics to prevent infection and external stitches will be taken out in a week. The internal ones will dissolve within two weeks. Physically, you will heal within two or three months and, mentally? Well, that depends on you.'

The room fell into silence.

The doctor looked at Eloise then at Anna and then back to James. 'I must remind you all that James is a very lucky man… considering.' After saying this, the doctor swiftly left the room, leaving the three of them to let all the information filter into their brains.

'So, I am a lucky man.' James muttered quietly.

'I didn't realise what those thugs actually did to you. I am so sorry James,' said Anna in a quivering voice. 'Is there anything that I can do?'

James thought for a moment. There were things that he desperately wanted to say but knew the futility of it. He would never regain her love but was grateful that at least she still cared about him. 'I will be fine. Honest,' was all that he could say.

'By the way, your boss rang earlier to say you can take as much time off as you need with full pay. He doesn't want you back until you have fully recovered,' Eloise informed him. 'Oh and your landlord, George and his wife Lily said they would not be able to visit you in hospital but will pop in every day when you get back to the flat. They will look after you and don't worry about the rent for now. That can be sorted out when you feel better.'

'Wow, you seem to have made quite an impression on certain people,' Anna sounded astonished but quickly realised that it seemed as if she could not imagine anyone liking him. Anna wanted to put aside any bad feelings that she was harbouring towards James because he did not deserve any of this. Also, now was not the time to upset him because it could interfere with his recovery.

'That is really kind of them.' James was overcome with emotion. Not everyone had turned their back on him. He still clung to the hope of one day proving his innocence to his family and being able to live freely, without the fear of being victimised ever again. However, he was not a police officer and did not know where to start. It did not help that there always seemed to be an obstacle preventing him from even trying. First, there was a lot to sort out after leaving prison. For instance, finding a place to live and getting a job; focusing on rebuilding a relationship with his children again. So far, he had made some progress with Eloise but failed to make any headway with his other two who refused to have anything to do with him. Now, this set back. It was frustrating but he had to do as he was told by the doctor in order regain his health and strength. Looking up at the ceiling, he made a short silent prayer. 'God, please grant me a miracle.'

CHAPTER EIGHTEEN

Before an unexpected visitor walked into Father Aiden's life, he was very happy being a priest, something that he always wanted to be since childhood. After he was ordained, this was his first parish that he was assigned to. At first, he felt out of his depth but after Adam's funeral, Father Aiden vowed that he would learn quickly and grow to fulfil his obligations as a good priest. He became inspired and was full of exciting ideas to lift his parish to new heights and took huge steps to win the respect and affection of his congregation. After all, he did have big shoes to fill. The previous long serving priest had won the hearts of the parishioners and when he died, it caused great mourning across the whole of the diocese. Numerous priests tried to take his place but could not settle and left very quickly. What the village needed was stability and that needed someone strong and willing to take the challenge. Somehow, the people felt that Father Aiden was the man that they were waiting for and once he settled, it did not take him long to form a good relationship with them and with every intention of remaining for the duration of time allocated by the bishop. As a result, the people in the village made more effort to get to know him and treated him amicably and with growing respect. Father Aiden was beginning to feel a wonderful sense of community and togetherness that was clearly lacking when he first arrived. This increased his sense of self-worth and confidence. He was actually enjoying his position as a priest. Who could have possibly foreseen that within moments of a woman walking into the church, it would change Father Aiden's life forever?

That morning, before this huge transformation in his life would take place, the day started as normal. He woke up to the sound of birds twittering in the nearby trees and a breeze was blowing through the open window, bringing a chill into the bedroom. He jumped out of bed and after washing and changing, he was ready to face the commitments made for the day. Father Aiden felt alive and youthful. He could not have been in a happier place if he tried. His life was content and fulfilled. Of course, he still felt sorrow and regret when he thought of Adam's suicide but the nightmares were already fading away. If so much could be achieved in such a short time then anything was possible.

His first task of the day was to thank the dedicated team of cleaners by giving them each a small box of chocolates. He then checked in his diary to see if there was anything that he had to do that day before preparing himself a hearty breakfast.

Just as he sat down to prepare a homily for the next Mass, there was a knock on the door. Surprised by the fact that it was only 8:45 in the morning, he looked towards the front door and frowned. Father Aiden put down the blank piece of paper that he was holding in his hand and swiftly made his way down the corridor. He opened the door to find an attractive lady standing on the door step. She was clasping her hands tightly in front of her chest and looked nervous. Her eyes were averted from him to avoid looking directly into his face. She looked kind and gentle but showed that something was deeply troubling her. Father Aiden noticing her agitation invited her in. Silently, Ashley entered the house and followed Father Aiden into the sitting room.

'How can I help you Miss?' asked Father Aiden.

'I'm Ashley, Ashley Davis, you may know my brother Tom and his wife Stacey?' Ashley's voice quivered as she spoke.

Father Aiden shook his head as he had never met any of the Davis family, however, he knew quite a lot about them and their tragic past. They were still the talk of the whole village which was to be expected. He was constantly told that they used to be enthusiastic church goers and were the centre of the community. They did a lot for charity, attending parish bazaars and contributing homemade cakes made by Alice, the mother. Michael, the father, never failed to play the part of Father Christmas in Santa's Grotto to give children a present. Father Aiden intended to visit all the family. He felt it was his duty to see Alice and Michael at their care homes and Tom and Stacey who stopped attending Sunday Mass. It would be wonderful if he could encourage them to come back. The problem was in finding the time do this because of the amount of work that had to be done within the parish.

'I need to make a confession Father,' Ashley reluctantly told him.

Since the day that Miss Colson had barged her way into his house demanding to take confession, Father Aiden had relaxed the rules. He now would take confession whenever a parishioner asked for one. It was one of the many conscious decisions he made in order to make up for his neglect in preventing Adam Bradshaw from taking his own life.

As he was looking at Ashley, he noticed that she had the same blank expression as Adam when he entered the sacristy and the resemblance made him shudder. She was Bradley Davis' sister and another strong connection with his death. Failing Adam was still eating at his conscience and the feeling of guilt was a furnace within his mind. He was not going to make that same mistake again. He had to get this one right. 'Ashley, please take a seat. We can talk in here. It will be more comfortable.' He tried to sound as welcoming and gentle as possible to put Ashley at ease. Father Aiden did not want her to change her mind and leave before telling him what was troubling her. Ashley took a step back, eyes wide like a timid rabbit, unsure whether to venture any closer into the room. Father Aiden definitely could not let this one escape, one false move and she would be lost. He needed to convince her that by talking to him about her problems, it would be the best remedy for making her feel better by unloading the pressure from within and letting it out onto someone completely neutral and with the integrity of keeping it in confidence. If he was able to make her feel secure enough to trust him then he could offer her hope and possibly guidance.

Ashley's eyes widened even more. 'No, no, not here. I don't want comfort. I don't deserve it. Once I tell you everything, you will think I'm a horrible person.' Her voice trembled and she fought back tears of shame. 'I want to do this the right way Father, in the confessional.'

'The confessional has not been used in years; the key has not been taken out of the side cupboard in ages.' Father Aiden was completely against the idea, imagining how musty it would smell inside.

'Father, please. I won't ask for forgiveness but I need to tell someone my secret before I explode.' Ashley grew firmer and more determined. 'I have been considering this carefully, thinking about it for many hours. I have not slept a wink last night. Yesterday, I made the most honest and good person to keep a secret from her husband. She truly did not want to do this. Believe me, it was a like asking her to kill someone.' Ashley stopped and held her hand to her mouth. For a moment, it looked as if she was going to be sick. 'I watched as she greeted her husband, my brother, with the guiltiest expression on her sweet face. The brightness in her eyes had died and seeing this made me realise that the truth that has been buried for a very long time had to be exposed. It can't go on. Something has to be done before it destroys yet another person in one way or another. God, I wish I never came back.'

'As you wish,' Father Aiden replied. He was willing to do anything to appease the poor woman. He turned towards the side cupboard and opened the first drawer. Ashley watched as he rustled around, pushing various items around until he found the key. As he pulled it out, she noticed that it was attached to a novelty key ring that read. 'Even Jesus loved his wine.' In different circumstances, this would have amused her but not that day. It must have belonged to the priest, Father Doolan, who was well known for his strange sense of humour. She remembered him from the days when she attended Mass. When she recently heard that Father Doolan died, the news saddened her but after thinking about this more clearly, it comforted her to know that he passed away peacefully in his sleep of old age. At least he did not suffer. Even though she was not a practising Catholic, she often thought about Father Doolan and his funny ways. It always managed to put a smile on her face except for now.

'Thank you,' Ashley whispered. She was trembling with fear but knew that she had to go through with it. However, the thought of what she was about to reveal was far worse than opening Pandora's Box. She was about to rip open the putrid, septic depths of hell that she was partly involved in, to her utter shame and despair.

'As I said, I don't expect forgiveness from you or God, I don't deserve it. I know that what I tell you will be in strictest confidence but what you decide to do with the information is totally up to you.'

Father Aiden frowned at her as she had him completely mystified and he found himself eager to know what it was that she was about to confess. Even though it sounded serious and extremely sinister, he did not fear listening to Ashley's confession but was surprised that it aroused his curiosity.

'I am ready,' Ashley's voice was thin and reedy and she was close to tears.

Father Aiden nodded and led the way to the main church. Once he reached the confessional, he opened the door and gestured for Ashley to enter through the door on the left while he went through the door on the right. A blast of damp air rushed out of the coffin like room and Father Aiden suddenly felt a sense of foreboding. He tried to hold his breath in an attempt to block the stale air from entering into his lungs and felt goose bumps all over his body. He could not fathom why he was reacting like this. For a brief moment Father Aiden hesitated and froze to the spot with panic. Once he gained control of himself, he reluctantly locked the door from the inside.

Once confession was over, Father Aiden watched as Ashley left the church. She did not turn around to look at him even once as she quickly walked down the aisle towards the porch door. When she opened it, the bright daylight wrapped around her form and engulfed her as she stepped into it. The door closed quietly behind her, shutting off the white light. Beads of sweat dotted his forehead and he rubbed them away with the back of his hand. What she had revealed was difficult for him to deal with and he was feeling giddy and nauseas by the revelation of pure evil. The law of the church forbids priests to reveal what they had learned during confession to anyone, even under the threat of their own death or that of others. For a priest to break confidentiality would lead to excommunication. Father Aiden was left with the dilemma of whether to abide by the rule of the church and live with the secret on his conscience or expose the truth and be damned forever. For the time being, he put his own predicament to one side and concentrated on Ashley. He was in two minds if to lay some of the blame on her because she should have confided in her parents. On the other hand she was a frightened child. When Ashley got older it became harder to open up to someone and she simply had to live with it on her conscience. He hoped that he gave her some solace but was not certain if he had. It was a heavy burden that Ashley carried. It would not be so simple to erase it from her mind. Father Aiden advised her to seek professional help because they would have the expertise and knowledge on how to deal with a situation like hers. In fact, he was very surprised that this kind of help was not provided for her in the first place and then the whole truth would have been slowly revealed. Ashley's mental and emotional state of mind had been overlooked and the poor girl had been let down by everyone. Her life might have been so different and that of others if people were not so busy with their own lives. Father Aiden was not certain what she would do but hoped that she would find the courage to take his advise and open up to a psychiatrist and perhaps end her torment.

For Father Aiden there would be a difficult choice to be made and he would have to do a lot of soul searching before reaching a decision. He moved towards the pews and clumsily fell into one of the benches. He knelt down and stared up at the crucifix that hung above the altar. He clasped his hands together, ready to pray. He gazed upon the gentle face of Jesus who appeared to look down at him with pity. His arms stretched out due to being pinned to a wooden cross. Father Aiden continued to study the Lord and found that the eyes were full of love and compassion.

'Oh dear God!' Father Aiden whispered frantically. 'Please tell me what I should do?'

CHAPTER NINETEEN

Miss Colson slowly levered herself up off the grass by clutching hold of the headstone and stretched. She vigorously rubbed the small of her back and winced as a sudden pain shot up her spine. She let out a heavy sigh as she looked around the graveyard. There was so much work to be done as weeds strangled the plants that had been planted during early spring and each headstone needed a good clean. The whole cemetery looked neglected and as a consequence failed miserably the loved ones that were buried. The only thing that cheered Miss Colson up was that the sun was shining brightly after many weeks of bad weather. It almost seemed like a miracle that the rays were so intense that they cut through the cold January air.

Earlier on, she had watched as the parish volunteers chatted and laughed amongst one another. They walked into the church in small groups or in pairs. Each one carried a cloth and detergent in a carrier bag ready to clean the church as well as the small meeting room that was built twenty years earlier. Miss Colson knew each and every one of those enthusiastic people comprised of both men and women, none of which were under the age of seventy five. Even in their old age, they were still spirited. Growing old taught them that life was too short to squander on being miserable but to make each day count and to live life to the full, grabbing each moment as though it was the last. They loved getting together and helping out with the work that needed to be done. It made them feel useful and young again by sharing their time together. They were more than happy to get up early in the morning, ready to start on the work.

Normally, Miss Colson would have joined them but at the end of each month, she made it her duty to clean at least a few of the headstones in the graveyard instead. The tasks that she had set for herself became more and more arduous because her bones and muscles ached whenever she tried to bend or get down onto her knees. It upset her how quickly she was becoming weaker with each passing year. However, she ignored the pain and dipped the sponge into the bucket of lukewarm soapy water and began to scrub the next headstone in line. Her knees whined as she knelt back down onto the cold, damp grass.

Miss Colson often reminisced over the times when she was a child when her mother frequently brought her here. She would take her by the hand and walk towards where Grandma and Granddad were buried to say some prayers and put flowers on their graves. Her mother always kept it tidy and told her that it was important not only to take care of your parents when they are alive but after they have died as well. They were the most important people in one's life and should remain so forever. They would also walk around the rest of the graves and her mother would read the inscriptions and tell her something about the people that she had liked and were once part of her life. Miss Colson never forgot the respect and loyalty her mother felt for them and wanted to do the same.

Miss Colson's mother passed away when she was only 18 years old. She found it difficult to accept that it did not take her father long before he married a woman a lot younger than himself. Miss Colson very quickly moved out from home because she could not watch her father with someone else when her mother's body was barely cold in the grave. She always thought that he was devoted to her mother but clearly, she must have been wrong. Miss Colson tried to avoid seeing her father, feeling that it would be for the best to save any aggravation. The only thing that his new wife and she had in common was the intense loathing that they felt towards one another.

Miss Colson never met a man that she wanted to marry and it never really bothered her. She was quite happy to make her own way in life. When Miss Colson was still young, she could never quite understand why people in the village should be so adamant in trying to find her a husband. For them getting married and having children was the most natural progression for a woman to make and if she insisted on remaining a spinster then she would end up being lonely and live a sad existence. Their view on life was totally different to hers. Why could they not understand that a woman could remain unmarried and still lead a fulfilling and happy life? Miss Colson personally, never had a problem with the prospect of staying single and that was possibly the reason why she could never form a loving relationship. She soon learnt from experience that many of the married women found themselves sooner or later on their own anyway. More often than not, when the husband died, the children were grown up by then and had no time for their mother because they had their own lives to lead. Marriage has never been a guarantee against loneliness. Now that she was old, she knew that it was the right avenue for her to take and she never regretted it for one single moment. She accumulated loads of good friends over the years with which she shared social events or just a natter over a cup of tea and cake. There was always plenty of work in the church that took a lot of her time. In fact, she was quite happy to occasionally have a quiet and restful time alone at home.

The only regret that she possibly had was not leaving the village in order to make a fresh start in London or even a foreign country. There was nothing to keep her in Punton when she was young. She was an intelligent and independent woman and there was a big wide world out there that she could have explored with all its possibilities. Miss Colson often wondered what kind of life she could have made for herself if only she had been a bit braver. Still there was no purpose for her to dwell on what could have been as life was kind to her and she thanked her lucky stars for it.

The stone she was now cleaning belonged to a soldier who died in 1940 during the evacuation of Dunkirk. The one behind, belonged to a young Corporal who died in Afghanistan. Nothing had changed during the ages because our soldiers are still fighting for a cause and proud to do so for their country. It gave her great pleasure to serve these brave men in her little way.

Time passed quickly for Miss Colson due to being busy and deep in her thoughts that when she looked towards the church, was surprised to see the cleaners leaving but with less energy this time. Nevertheless, they were still smiling with the satisfaction of knowing that they did their bit for the community. They passed without even giving a quick glance towards the graveyard and therefore, did not see her looking in their direction. She placed the sponge into the bucket, bowed her head and silently prayed for all of the departed in the graveyard with an extra special prayer for her mother and family. This was a ritual that she observed every time she finished cleaning the headstones.

Miss Colson then picked up the bucket which was heavy with dirty water and started to walk towards the church. The bucket swung from side to side, sloshing around and spilling over the sides from time to time. When Miss Colson reached the side of the church, she was able to pour the dirty water into the drain and clean the bucket with water from the tap. While she was doing this, the sound of a car could be heard pulling up into the church driveway. Miss Colson stopped to see who could be visiting at such an early hour. It was only 8.45 and Mass would not start until 10 o'clock. Father Aiden would now be having his breakfast. She frowned, astonished to see that it was Ashley Davis walking towards the manse, obviously wanting to see Father Aiden. She had stopped going to church years ago when her brother died and on her return from Australia, only came once and that was to Adam's funeral. Ashley did not even know Father Aiden so why would she want to see him? This seemed very odd indeed.

Miss Colson continued to observe Ashley and noticed that she was not walking with her normal self-assurance but with her head bent down. Even from this distance, she could see that the young woman was nervous and terribly upset. Miss Colson was instantly curious and could not help but to want to know what was going on. Even though her body was aching, she decided to stay a little longer to scrub some more stones. That way she would see Ashley leaving the house. Once Miss Colson filled the bucket, she ambled back to the graveyard. After a few steps, she would stop, place the bucket on the ground and stand there, huffing and puffing until her heartbeat had the time to return to a slower rhythm. Once she felt able to continue, she picked up the bucket and moved on, until she had to rest again.

As Miss Colson carried on cleaning, she glanced back towards the church from time to time. She did not want to miss seeing Ashley leave. Time seemed to be passing slowly and Miss Colson was feeling very thirsty and tired. She wondered how long she would have to wait until Ashley emerged from the house. At least she could be thankful for the mild weather. So Miss Colson found herself walking back and forth, filling the bucket until finally after the third time, she heard footsteps leaving the church. She wondered why Ashley had gone into the house only to exit through the front door of the church. She was moving quickly, making a crunching noise on the gravel. Miss Colson watched, as still as a statue, as Ashley paused to look back at the church. Ashley caught sight of

Miss Colson and stared for a few seconds. She did not wave or acknowledge Miss Colson in any way but swiftly made her way back to the car. Once Ashley was inside, she appeared to be speaking to someone on her mobile phone. Then revving up the engine and within a blink of an eye, she had driven through the front gates and was gone.

Miss Colson dropped the bucket on the ground and shivered. Even at this distance, she could see that something was terribly wrong and it worried her. There was always something strange about that family, especially after the poor child's tragic death and what she had just witnessed, disturbed her for some reason. She gazed upon the church and wondered if Father Aiden might need some help. Whatever went on between the two of them in there, it surely could not have been anything but unpleasant.

She was no longer curious but concerned and decided to make her way towards the church with haste; she walked across the grass until she reached the pathway that led to the front door. Once there, she turned the iron handle and let herself in. She stopped when she reached the back of the aisle and saw Father Aiden kneeling over the front pew. He had his back to her but she could hear by his plea to God for help that he was very distressed.

Slowly and quietly, she stepped towards him and once she was by his side, carefully placed her hand gently on his shoulder, 'Father?' she whispered.

Father Aiden took his hands away from his face and looked up at her with his puffy red eyes. He then grabbed hold of her hand and stood up sharply, pulling her close to him and hugging her tightly. At first this shocked Miss

Colson, who was brought up never to get too familiar with a priest and she stiffened.

'Really need to talk to you.' Father Aiden murmured.

Miss Colson's heart melted with each word that he spoke and steadily let him hold on to her as she stroked his head like a consoling mother. They stayed like that for some time until Father Aiden was able to pull himself together just enough to make his way back into the lounge.

As he sat on the settee, Miss Colson opened the cupboard in the kitchen and reached her hand into the back of it, to see if there was any more hidden treats left inside. To her relief there was a brand new bottle of brandy that had not yet been opened. She considered whether to add it to coffee but instead, opened the bottle, retrieved two small glasses, and filled them to the top with the potent liquid while thinking to herself, 'So what if it is early in morning, Father Aiden needs a drink and to be honest, so do I.' When she got to the lounge she placed one on the table next to him and sat in the arm chair opposite, still holding on to the other glass. She took a sip and felt it heat up her lips, coat her tongue with fire and like molten lava, slip down her throat. She waited patiently for the priest to speak.

'I don't know where to start.' Father Aiden told her. His voice was without any emotion. He felt completely drained.

'From the beginning is usually the best.' Miss Colson suggested. She took another sip of her drink and placed it on the sideboard next to her seat.

Father Aiden sighed heavily. 'Something awful has happened and I don't know what to do about it.' He shook his head and wiped his lips nervously. 'In law it states that if you have first-hand knowledge of a criminal act then you are legally bound to report it to the police. If you don't then you are perverting the course of justice or something like that.'

Miss Colson nodded but frowned. She was not sure where this was all leading to.

'If a person came to you and told you about a crime so vile that it badly affected the lives of many people and kept secret for years, what would you do?' Father Aiden stared at Miss Colson as he said this. It made her feel uncomfortable as his expression was full of expectancy. He hoped that her answer would solve all of his problems.

Miss Colson bowed her head in thought. She knew that she would have to be very careful with her answer. Finally, she looked back at the pitiful man before her and said, 'Father, am I right to assume that what you have been told was in the strictest confidence?'

Father Aiden nodded and replied, 'Confession.'

Miss Colson's eyes widened and she gasped. 'Am I right in thinking that someone came to you, seeking help or advice through confession this morning?' She was starting to piece things together.

'Yes. It was...' Father Aiden was ready to tell her everything.

'I really do not want to know.' Miss Colson stopped him curtly. 'I have full respect that a confession is shared with a priest in the strictest confidence, Father. I have no right to be given any details.'

'So, you think I should not go to the police with what I know?' Father Aiden clearly wanted to be advised by Miss Colson on what he should do.

Miss Colson was stunned. 'Father, you do realise that no matter how terrible the sin might be, it was confessed with the trust that you, as a man of God, would not break the law of the church by divulging it. If priests started to break such a sacred trust, then how could we keep our faith in the church? The rules of the church must be obeyed no matter what. If anyone tried to bend them for their own convenience then it would make a mockery of the whole establishment.'

Father Aiden listened to her every word carefully, considering each point that she made. He then looked out of the window for a moment; there was so much to think about and he had to be very sure in making the right decision. He returned his attention to the patient woman and said, 'Miss Colson, you do not know the gravity or seriousness of the confession. You cannot come to a conclusion so easily.'

'And would it be so easy for you to turn your back on the priesthood? You know what it would mean if you break Ashley's trust.'

Father Aiden's mouth fell open, he did not realise that Miss Colson saw her leave just a few minutes ago.

Miss Colson continued. 'If you break Ashley's trust, you will lose your position as a priest and possibly be excommunicated. Could you really live with that?'

'I know what you are saying but I am so unsure where my loyalties should lie at this moment. People have the right to know the truth, believe me.' Father Aiden was determined to convince her. He had never felt so lost, so confused in all of his life. Within a space of an hour he learnt so much about himself, things that he did not like. He could despise another human being to the point of abomination. He was unable to provide comfort and words of wisdom about the everlasting love of God. Most of all, he was weak, so weak that he had to take shelter in the arms of the parishioner that he most adored and respected. He needed to be mothered like a small child. He was not a good priest, he was not even worthy to be called a man.

Miss Colson picked up her glass and drank the remaining liquor. She grimaced and then returned the empty glass to its place. 'Father Aiden, you are not thinking clearly right now and that is a fact. I will always respect any decision that you make and will always be your friend. Make sure that what you choose to do is right for you.' Saying this, she got up and this time winced as her muscles intensely ached. 'It would be a huge pity if Punton lost the best priest it ever had.' She smiled sympathetically and made her way to the front door.

She stepped outside and let the breeze rush over her face. She then looked up to the sky and saw that it was a beautiful shade of light blue. Only a few white clouds were dotted here and there. For a moment, she smiled at how extraordinary the world was but then felt guilty when she thought about the conversation she just had with Father Aiden. She instantly stopped smiling and muttered, 'Dear Lord, help his wretched soul.' She then slowly made her way back home feeling downcast.

CHAPTER TWENTY

As Ashley emerged from the church and closed the door gently behind her, she sighed with relief. In the past hour she had gone through the most difficult moral task imaginable. As a child she had never really taken confession all that seriously and felt that she had to make up a list just to have something to tell the priest. Today, however, was completely different. She felt damned, unclean and ashamed. After the whole family had stopped going to church soon after Bradley's death, Ashley never gave another thought about her Catholic upbringing or in fact God himself. Now that she had to stand and face a priest, a sense of fear and respect sprung up from within her. The presence of Father Aiden magnified the guilt that she felt for all of those years. This was the reason why she had insisted on using the confessional instead of sitting opposite the priest in the lounge. That was far too informal for her liking and she did not want to say all those awful things while sitting directly in front of him, face to face. She preferred to say her confession from behind a wooden wall.

Ashley despised her brother even more than ever for putting her through all this. Although, she felt emotionally drained and completely exhausted, she knew that there was one more thing that she had to do and that was to confront her brother, Tom. By some chance, he was working from home and Stacey would be at work. This would give her the opportunity that she needed to speak to him alone.

Late last night, whilst everyone was asleep, she booked herself a ticket for a flight back to Australia for today at 2.45 pm. She then, quietly packed her bags and placed them in the cupboard ready for when she would make a quick exit out of the house.

Ashley had just confessed her secret to Father Aiden and was now ready for the next part of her plan. It was now 9.45 am and Ashley started walking towards the car when suddenly she caught something moving in the corner of her eye. She turned towards the graveyard and saw Miss Colson standing by one of the graves. She had a bucket by her side and was staring straight at her with her mouth wide open. Ashley's eyes narrowed. She remembered Miss Colson from her childhood and knew that she had a reputation of being a busy body and a judgemental cow. It then came to Ashley's mind that Miss Colson would have a shock if she knew what she had just told Father Aiden. She then swiftly turned away and headed towards her car. Once Ashley got in, she took out her mobile phone and rang the car hire firm to pick the car up from the airport. She still needed it to drive to the airport and after that they could have it back. Ashley then put the engine on and with all haste drove to Tom's house. She had worked out that it would take her an hour and a half to get to the airport and had to be there two hours in advance before departure. That would give her enough time to face up to Tom and challenge him about Bradley. Once that was over, she would fetch the luggage from the cupboard and leave without delay. She did not know what to expect from the outcome of their confrontation but was positive that it had to be done. If she failed to go through with it, she would never be able to feel good about herself for the rest of her life. Since returning to England, it had all been a complete nightmare and it had to end in one way or another.

Ashley finally reached her destination and pulled up onto the drive. As Ashley stepped out of the car she could hear her heart pounding and was feeling so weak that she held onto the car door for a few moments to give herself time to recover. Ashley knew that she should have done this years ago but was too scared to go through with it before. She ran away to live in Australia simply to escape from her brother and the turmoil that he caused in her life. Tom was like a nasty disease that infected the people around him that he touched. Now she had the strength and was ready to strike at the heart of the contamination and hopefully cleanse her own soul.

Closing her eyes, Ashley tried to steady herself. Her head was spinning round and she felt faint. Breathing in deeply, she felt the blood rush back to her head and started to feel better and calmer. She had to be strong and not falter. This was her moment to fight back and she did not want to ruin it in any way. With determination in her steps, she marched to the front door, took the key out from her bag and without any hesitation, opened the front door.

'Ashley, where have you been? You left without any breakfast,' Stacey's voice showed concern.

Ashley frowned and was completely confused. 'Aren't you working today? Your car…'

'Since I knew that Tom was going to be home today, which rarely happens these days, I thought that it would be nice if I stayed home too. I will be able to make him a lovely lunch and be on standby whenever he wants some coffee. Oh, and I put my car in the garage to give you extra space. Makes sense since I am not using it until tomorrow,' Stacey chirped. Then she looked at Ashley closely and noticing her agitation asked in a more serious tone, 'Did you take my advice then?'

Ashley regarded her friend sympathetically for a moment and then replied, 'Stacey, I am so sorry but there is something unpleasant that I must do. I was hoping to spare you from this but you deciding to stay home might have turned out for the best. You won't like it but you have every right to hear what I have to say to Tom.' She tipped her head in the direction of Tom's office and deliberately raising her voice said, 'I did go to see the priest this morning and confessed all the sins that I had committed years ago. In fact thirty years ago to be exact and I left nothing out.'

Stacey bit her bottom lip, stunned by the intensity in Ashley's voice. She knew that Tom was far too busy to be disturbed and yet it was obvious from Ashley's tone that this was exactly what she intended to do.

'What has this got to do with Tom?' Stacey asked in a pitiful voice.

Ashley returned her attention to her friend. 'I'm afraid my dear one, it has everything to do with Tom.' She watched as Tom stepped out of his office into the corridor, standing a few feet away from her.

'Yes Ashley, what has this got to do with me?' He asked as if he had no idea what all the commotion was about.

Ashley could not believe her brother's complacency towards the whole situation. She was just about to expose their darkest secret in front of Stacey and he seemed unfazed by it all. He was actually smiling smugly with his hands in his pockets. As he glared at her, Ashley could actually read his thoughts. If there was a thought bubble above his head, it would read, 'Go on then, out with it… I dare you!'

Seeing his cockiness only created a burning sensation in the pit of her stomach and as she watched him slowly nodding his head, the sensation ignited into a raging inferno. Instead of backing down, Ashley burst out, 'Tom killed Bradley.'

An eerie kind of silence followed. Ashley stood completely still; her eyes were wide as she gaped at Tom. This was not how she had envisaged starting the conversation. She did not expect to just come out with it like that. However, there it was, the black cloud that was hanging over them burst open, allowing the tension and rage that was building up, to be finally set free.

Tom stared at Ashley with a comical look of surprise on his face. He was so sure that because his sister felt partly to blame, she would never be brave enough to divulge what really happened to Bradley. He turned to look at Stacey, who was also gaping in astonishment at Ashley. None of them spoke for a while, just stood there motionless.

Eventually, Stacey whined, 'Tom? What does she mean?'

Tom failed to reply but lowered his head. Ashley knew him well enough to know that his reaction was not from feeling ashamed or guilty but from being found out. Tom could barely look at his wife, the one person who really mattered to him. He knew that his marriage could possibly be over.

'The four of us, Tom, Adam, Bradley and me went out to play in the snow. Tom killed my little brother.' Ashley explained as if she was in a trance. It was still vivid in her mind.

Stacey continued to stare at Ashley and then shook her head slowly. She began to chuckle which turned into a hysterical laugh. 'That's absurd. Ashley, what are you on?'

It was Tom who spoke next confirming, 'It's true.'

Stacey turned to face him. The look of love had vanished and was replaced by one of revulsion. 'Why?' she asked quietly, still trying to make sense of the whole thing.

Tom gave a deep sigh and then began to talk, 'When it was just me and Ashley, everything was great. Both Mum and Dad adored me and showered all their attention on me. Ashley was a sweet girl who looked up to me.' Both women listened intently to what he was saying. 'When Bradley came along that all changed. It was Bradley this and Bradley that. Look how cute he is, how wonderful he is. God, it made me sick.' The frustration and bitterness that Tom felt as a child resurfaced and he began to shuffle from one foot to the other with aggravation. 'Mum and Dad no longer doted on me like they once did and even Ashley spent more time playing with Bradley.'

'I still idolised you after Bradley was born. Don't bring me into your self-pity.'

'Don't think for one minute that you are the innocent one in all this.' Stacey angrily lashed out at Ashley. 'You were there. You could have done something to save Bradley or at least said something years ago. I can't believe that we sat for hours having so many discussions and you never once thought to tell me all this? You were even happy to put the blame on James Dickson. Remember how you consoled me last night? How could you? You are just as much to blame as Tom.'

Ashley took a step back but said nothing. In a way everything that Stacey was saying was true.

Tom frowned but chose to continue with his story. 'That day in particular, Bradley was being more annoying than ever. I didn't even want to take him with us. It was meant to be Adam, you and me, like it always had been in the past whenever it snowed. That time, Mum thought it would be good if we included Bradley. He moaned about everything; he was cold, he was bored, he was hungry.'

'He was only five years old,' Ashley muttered.

'Yes he was only five, not old enough to be going out to play in the snow with us.' Tom barked angrily. 'He vexed me and so needed to be dealt with.'

Stacey could not believe what she was hearing. Worst of all Tom showed no sign of remorse. 'You brutally murdered your brother. How demented are you?' she spat.

Tom rapidly batted his eyelids and then carried on trying to explain, 'I was only a child myself at that time, Stacey. We all make mistakes when we are children.'

Stacey shook her head and cried, 'No! No! You were old enough to know exactly what you were doing and what about all those years of hiding your evil deed. An innocent man spent thirty years of his life in prison and lost his family in the process. Your mother ended up in a mental institution and your father lost his beloved wife.' She paused for a moment to gather her thoughts. 'In fact, you ruined the lives of many people. Your jealousy destroyed everything.'

Tom stepped towards Stacey with his arms out to embrace her in the hope of appeasing her.

'Don't you dare come any closer to me. Our marriage is over, not that it was ever real. It was all a farce. I didn't know you at all. You are a stranger to me.' Now she was close to tears.

Tom clutched his heart with his hand and with real emotion choked, trying to hold back his tears. 'Stacey, I am the same man you swore to love and honour for the rest of your life. I sincerely and truly love you and always will. We can get over this and become even stronger.'

'You know nothing about love, you're simply a shell without a heart, incapable of any emotion.' Stacey vehemently threw back at him. 'I shudder to think that for years I let you touch me, kiss me… God, I feel queasy just thinking about it. And what if we had a child together? I am so glad you are impotent. So, stay right where you are, I don't ever want you near me again.'

'I never killed anyone else, I swear.' Tom replied with conviction. He was quite satisfied that he only did it the once.

Stacey glared and huffed at him with disbelief. 'Can't you even hear yourself?' She raised her hands in the air gesturing that she had given up. 'I never want to see you ever again. I want you out of my life, do you hear me?'

Ashley cut in saying, 'And neither do I.' She could see Stacey opening her mouth to say something but stopped her by quickly adding, 'Stacey, I know you hate me right now and I don't blame you. I hate myself, believe me. I'm going back home to Australia today. I just need to collect my bags from my room and I'm gone. This time it's for good.' On this note, she stomped up the stairs. After a few minutes, she came back down, carrying the heavy cases.

Neither Stacey nor Tom moved to help her but watched as she struggled to the front door. Before leaving, she turned to Tom for the last time and said, 'Remember, Father Aiden knows everything. How long will it be before everyone else knows too?'

Ashley slammed the door behind her, leaving Tom and Stacey standing in silence, listening to the car engine revving and the wheels screeching as it pulled out off the drive. They remained completely still until it faded into the distance. Ashley was gone.

Tom looked at Stacey and tried to move a little closer to her.

'Don't even think about it, you bastard.' Then Stacey did something that even shocked her. She swung her arm right back and gathering momentum with all her strength, thrust her fist forward until it smashed into Tom's face. She missed his cheek and hit his nose. The huge diamond ring that he gave her for Christmas, sliced into his nostrils. Blood gushed out dripping onto his shirt and carpet floor. Tom, now in terrible pain, stared at her like a wounded animal. Stacey held her hands over her mouth and then walked out of the front door and slammed it shut in the same way as Ashley did a moment ago. She did not know where she was going but just needed to get away from the house. She could no longer breathe in the same air as Tom.

CHAPTER TWENTY-ONE

FATHER AIDEN STARED at the blank sheet of paper in front of him. He wanted to compose a letter to Miss Colson, letting her know what he had decided to do about Ashley's confession. The problem was that he had been sitting at his desk, nervously tapping his pen on the table for the past half hour but could not find the right words to put on the paper.

When Father Aiden first met Miss Colson, he found her to be a nuisance and an irritating gossip. How quickly that all changed once he got to know her better. Now, she was his confidante and best friend. He learnt that Miss Colson was interested in the lives of the people living around her and she liked to talk about them but never with the intention of being nasty. Miss Colson was glad when life was going well for the people around her but concerned when they had problems. Father Aiden believed her to be kind, honest and trustworthy but badly misunderstood by many of the villagers in Punton because she was forthright and never afraid to speak her mind. Most people in life want to be told only what they want to hear. Keeping to this philosophy allows for a quiet life without making enemies. Miss Colson was different, although her directness offended many people; she was quite prepared in accepting their candidness towards her. Miss Colson had strong principles and he could only hope that she would respect his decision and continue to be his friend. So, he just stared at the wretched piece of paper not knowing where to start. It was proving to be one of the most difficult letters for Father Aiden to write because it was important for him to explain the essential part that she played in his life and how much he valued her friendship.

After Miss Colson had left the previous morning, Father Aiden had remained in the lounge. Picking up his glass of untouched brandy, he swallowed all of its contents in one go. This was done absently and he barely felt the heat of the liquor burn its way down his throat. He looked around at the many photographs that he had carefully placed on the walls. Each one reminded him of the good times that he shared with the community of Punton such as baptisms and weddings. Occasionally, he was invited to a birthday party or a celebration of some kind. In every single one of them, he was surrounded by grinning faces of all the amazing individuals that he grew to love. In such a short space of time, he too touched many lives and gained their respect and trust.

He thought back to Miss Colson's parting words that were kind yet heart breaking. In a sweet and gentle voice she said, 'It would be a huge pity if Punton lost the best priest it ever had.' What a wonderful thing to say, Father Aiden thought to himself and as he gazed at the photographs on the wall, he realised that there could be some truth in her comment. In spite of that, he had to give up and leave the priesthood for good. From hereon, he would be remembered as just another priest who abandoned the village. That was the reason why Father Aiden also felt the pain in Miss Colson's words; he had promised to be faithful to his flock and now he was leaving them. Perhaps they would come to understand that it was for them that he was doing this. It would stop their hatred and vengeance towards an innocent man and in turn James and his family could live in peace. He had to give up what he most loved for the good of the village people. If not the church, God would surely forgive him for this.

That afternoon Father Aiden was holding the phone in his hand to ring his parents to give them the bad news. He knew that it would be very difficult for them to accept his decision. He was not looking forward to telling them but decided that it would be for the best if he did it straight away.

His parents were devout members of the Catholic Church and had lived their entire lives following its teachings faithfully and without question. Their belief was strong and nothing would ever change that. When Aiden had announced that he was going to join the priesthood, they were ecstatic and proud. He remembered how his father shook his hand and then grabbed him tightly into his arms after realising that he was being too formal towards his beloved son. His mother jumped up and down screaming with joy and clapped her hands. When his father finally let go of him, his mother took her turn, loudly proclaiming that Aiden had definitely secured his seat next to God in heaven. Even now, he could clearly see her winking and smiling cheekily at him saying, 'And your prayers will surely secure our entrance to heaven so that we can be there with you. God would not want to separate a loving family, now would he?'

When Father Aiden was ordained, he went back to his parents for a short stay. The day he left for his first placement which was in Punton, his mother cried from joy because her dear son was going to do God's work. She packed a huge amount of sandwiches, homemade casseroles and soups that he could freeze once he arrived at his new home. His mother also packed a variety of cakes assuring him that they could also be frozen as she had baked them all that very morning.

When he was driving off in the taxi, he waved them a goodbye until they were out of sight. Father Aiden remembered smiling because he had begun his incredible journey towards a new life. Who would have thought at that time how it would all end up?

He stood there for a while, holding the telephone in his hand, dreading to make the call. Once he dialled the number there would be no going back. His mother picked up the phone and could hardly contain her excitement at hearing his voice. He could hear her shouting to his father, 'It's Aiden on the phone.'

As his mother's bubbly voice rattled on about the numerous exciting things that had happened at home, Father Aiden listened whilst the knife twisted round and round in his heart. He was about to rip his parents world into shreds. Their wonderful son had failed them and everyone else. He was going to break one of the most sacred rules of the church by telling the police everything that he was told in the confessional about Bradley's death. Then he heard her say, 'Oh just listen to me going on. So what about you Aiden, are things okay?'

Father Aiden paused for a moment, realising there was no way that he could tell his mother what he was about to do over the phone. This needed to be said face to face once the deed was done. 'I'm coming home Ma,' was all he could manage to say. He was all choked up after hearing his mother's voice.

He could hear the commotion on the other side of the telephone as his mother happily called out to his father saying, 'Aiden is coming home to see us, how wonderful is that?' Then she returned her attention back to her son and asked, 'When should we be expecting you?'

'Tomorrow, early afternoon,' Father Aiden replied and put the phone down.

There was so much for him to do before then. He would go to the police station in town first thing in the morning and then make that dreadful phone call to the bishop. Initially, he intended to have the courtesy of informing the bishop before going to the police station but knew that he would do everything in his power to stop him. He was not going to allow anyone to try and change his mind. An innocent man had lost thirty years of his life and was still living in torment. He had seen what happened to him on the news and it filled him with utter despair. It was up to him to put things right for James Dickson and his family and no-one was going to get in his way. He was aware that he was about to lose everything that mattered to him but was willing to make that sacrifice because what James Dickson and his family went through, outweighed the sufferance that he was about to subject himself to. For a brief moment, he compared himself to Jesus, sacrificing himself for the sake of others but quickly brushed it aside for fear of being blasphemous.

That day, he missed all of his appointments and failed to answer the door when anyone knocked. Father Aiden could not face any of his parishioners because of what he was about to do and in theory, he was no longer their priest. Instead, he turned his attention to packing his bags. Father Aiden knew that once he rang the bishop, he would have to leave immediately. He would be replaced by someone temporary until they found a new parish priest.

After a long, agonising time of staring at the blank piece of paper, Father Aiden stopped tapping the pen and began to write.

Dear Miss Colson,

He stopped, read the first three words and then crumpled the paper and chucked it in the bin. It bounced off the side and fell to the floor. Taking another sheet, he started again.

My dearest friend,

He felt that was much better, so he continued.

> *I am very grateful for everything that you have done for me. You have been my guide, my friend, and an angel sent by God to watch over me. I cannot find the words to express how much your friendship has meant to me. Believe me; it has taken over half an hour for me to even make a start on this letter because it meant a lot to me to get it right.*

Since I came to Punton, I feel that I have grown and risen to the challenge of becoming a good priest and that would not have been possible without you by my side. Your understanding and patience gave me comfort in my hour of need after Ashley's confession. It would have been difficult for me to have faced my lowest point in my life alone. You were there to console and support me. In circumstances like this, I would usually turn to my mother but it was not possible on that occasion. Instead of my mother you were there like a guardian angel, allowing me to talk through with you my dilemma until I knew exactly what I had to do. This raised my spirits and gave me courage to do what I feel; the right thing.

I believe, the least I can do after you patiently listened to my predicament, is to let you know of my decision. I thought long and hard about this and held your advice close to my heart but at the end of the day, I felt that it was my duty to go to the police with the information that was given to me in confidence during confession. You quite rightly did not want the details of what was said and I respect you for that. It will all become clear to you soon once it is reported on the news. I am sure that I will be cast out from the Catholic Church which has always been the centre of my existence. Hopefully, the people of Punton might find it in their hearts to forgive me. Most of all, I sincerely pray that you will be able to see the good side of this damned soul and continue to be my friend.

Peace be with you.
Aiden.

He could no longer bring himself to using the title of Father. That part of his life was now over. Aiden did not believe that a new hopeful chapter would begin. There would be nothing left for him to look forward to but emptiness.

He then placed the letter into an envelope. Sighing heavily, he placed a first class stamp on it and stood up. He glanced at his luggage then made his way to the front door.

Aiden left the parish church dressed in a plain t-shirt and jeans, and made his way to the bus stop. On the way there, he dropped the letter into the mailbox. When the bus arrived, he quietly paid his fare and headed into town towards the police station.

CHAPTER TWENTY-TWO

AFTER STACEY SLAMMED the door behind her, she took her hands away from her mouth and screamed. She did not care that her next door neighbour, who had been fetching something from the glove compartment, had bumped his head on his car door and was now rubbing it gently whilst staring at her in surprise. She kept on screaming until she had no breath left. She slumped down on the front doorstep and threw her arms around her raised knees and rocked back and forth in a crouched position. Tears streamed down her face and her whole body shook uncontrollably. Everything that Ashley had said, replayed back in her mind and she found it impossible to make sense of it all. Her husband, whom she had loved and adored for so many years, was a demon. He had killed his own brother and even now felt no remorse for doing it.

Like photographs in an album, she was turning the pages in her mind of her life with Tom. She had images of her wedding day; buying a house; kissing under the mistletoe at Christmas and dancing intimately on the beach until sunset. Stacey's memories no longer made her feel warm and happy inside like they used to but turned her stomach with revulsion until finally, she leaned forward and threw up. Once she was done, she sat back and stared at the mess on the paved ground and wiped her mouth with the back of her hand.

All this time her neighbour watched in silence as he was standing next to his car. He was not sure what to do. He slowly advanced towards her and moved his mouth as if he was about to say something but stopped when Stacey began to vomit. Looking down at the mess in disgust, thinking that she was drunk, quickly turned back and went inside his house.

Stacey knew that Tom must have heard her screaming outside the door but decided to keep out of her way. This came as no surprise to her when only moments ago, she hit him in the face with all her might. She abhorred violence but got herself into such a frenzy losing control of her senses and lashed out. Stacey would never forget Tom's face as he looked at her shocked and profoundly hurt. Stacey felt alarmed at the way she behaved as it was against all her beliefs. Her negative reaction to Tom brought her no comfort but sadness that she caused him pain. Her marriage to him was over. She would never take him back. The tragedy of it was that she still loved him. One cannot easily rip someone they adore from their heart. Hopefully with the passing of time, her love for Tom will wither and die.

Stacey shook her head and sighed. How could life be so cruel? One moment there was nothing but bliss and the next; grief. She had no idea that morning, when she got out of bed that it would end up like this. Stacey wiped away her tears and stood up. There was no time for self-indulgence. She had some important news to tell James Dickson so there was no time to lose. Stacey opened the garage door, got into her car and drove straight to the hospital.

Even though James served his thirty years sentence, the protesters waiting outside on the day of his release showed him no mercy. He was branded a murderer for a crime that he did not commit. James came out of one jail only to enter into another. Stacey wanted to give him back a new lease of life. He had the right to know who was responsible for Bradley's death and tell the world that he was innocent. Tom would get what he deserves.

The traffic was slow on the outskirts of the town and it would take her a while before she would reach the hospital. It gave Stacey a little bit of time to think over things. If she told James the truth then Tom's family would also be drawn into this mess. Ashley was on her way to the airport and no longer cared about the mayhem that she had left behind but what about their mother and father? How would they feel if they found out that their eldest son killed his brother? It would destroy them. They already had a cross to bear, why add to their suffering? They were now old and perhaps it would be kinder if the secret could be kept hidden for a little longer. She still felt that it was her duty to tell James but would ask him for the sake of Tom's innocent family, if he could keep the truth to himself. Deep down, she felt that James would grant her the wish. Stacey obviously knew that she was not a good judge of character after her complete trust in Tom but was certain that James was a kind and honest man and would not have the heart to let her down. However, if somehow the truth got out, then she would gladly see James shouting from the highest mountain that he was innocent.

Stacey reached the hospital and to her delight found a space to park her car. Visiting James was helping her to take her mind off her own problems. As she approached the reception desk, to her astonishment, she felt weak at the knees and she could feel herself trembling. Her hands were clasped together and she began to take short, sharp breaths. The receptionist looked up at her and it was obvious by her sympathetic expression that she could see that Stacey was feeling nervous, 'How can I help you?' the receptionist asked in a sweet and calming tone.

Stacey took another deep breath and almost whispering replied, 'I would like to know which ward James Dickson is in please?'

The receptionist turned towards her computer screen and started to tap loudly on the keys. 'Friend or relative?' she asked, more out of curiosity than necessity.

'Neither,' Stacey was quick to answer. She then looked down at the floor and changed her mind. 'Friend, I guess.'

The receptionist smiled and looked back at Stacey who had grown quite pale and seemed on the verge of tears. 'I am sure your friend is okay. He is now allowed to have visitors which means he is on the road to recovery. It is the Bluebell Ward, on the third floor. The lift is just ahead of you.'

'Thanks.' Stacey forced a smile.

When Stacey reached the door to the Bluebell Ward, she had to click a button to enter. There she found another reception desk but this time a nurse was standing behind the counter. The nurse was not as pleasant as the receptionist and with a dour face asked, 'Who have you come to see?'

Stacey replied, 'Mr Dickson.'

'You will find him in room 5. It's down the corridor on the left.' After that she looked straight at her computer.

Stacey, without another word, walked towards the direction of where she would find James. She passed the wards on the way and glanced inside. There were rows of beds filled with people who were either lying down or sitting in chairs, propped up by white, starched pillows. Some of them slept while others moaned in pain. There were also patients who were happily chatting away to their friends and loved ones. Towards the end of the corridor there were separate rooms which were only available for those who paid extra for the privacy. James on the other hand, would be in one of those rooms due to the extensive injuries he had sustained and because he was known to most of the patients as the man who killed a sweet, young boy named Bradley Davis. His presence on a ward could mean trouble from angry visitors and patients who would be more than happy to beat him up or some of them would feel extremely uncomfortable with his presence in the room. It was best to keep James separate and avoid any trouble or discomfort.

The door to his room was open and Stacey could clearly see James who was sitting up on his bed talking to a pretty young lady. There was also an attractive older woman with them, sitting a bit further away in a chair with her arms folded, staring into space. The younger lady was completely focused on James and was now fussing with his bed sheets and pillows.

Stacey slowly entered the room and just stood there staring at James not knowing what to say or do. As soon as he noticed Stacey, he beckoned her to come closer. Stacey was aware that James would be covered with cuts and bruises but was not prepared for this. His face was so swollen that his whole head appeared misshapen. His eyes looked like slits from being badly puffed up and were seeping in the corners. He was barely recognisable but she knew that it was him from the moment she saw him. Perhaps it was his movements or the thickness and colour of his hair that poked through the blood stained bandages. He tried desperately to smile but it ended up looking comical and insane all at the same time. Slowly he shook his head because he could not believe that she had come to visit him. 'Stacey, what a surprise,' struggling with every word he said.

The young lady turned to look at Stacey and gave a warm smile. The other woman frowned, curious to know who she was.

Stacey looked from one woman to the other and then said to James, 'There is something I need to tell you.'

James cocked his head to one side and indicated for her to go on.

'I know that you did not kill Bradley Davis that day in the snow.' She paused and took a deep breath. 'It was his brother Tom. He told me today. One big request I do have from all of you. For the sake of his mother and father, please find it in your hearts to keep this secret to yourselves; at least for now.'

Silence swept into the room and held everyone captive. It hovered over the four of them, paralysing each one until James suddenly clutched his head and let out a hoarse cry that tumbled out from the very pit of his stomach. They all looked at him in alarm. They were unsure if he had gone insane. James' cry was unlike any other they had heard before. His frustration, anger, hurt and despair was released in one swoop from his fragile body. After this he said with joy, 'God has answered my prayer.' James suddenly began to cough, grabbing hold of his chest and shouting, 'Oh it hurts, it hurts'.

Eloise quickly snapped out of her bewilderment and gave her father some water to drink.

He gazed adoringly at Stacey and said, 'The miracle that I have been hoping for has happened.' Tears of joy cascaded down his cheeks. This amazing woman has given him the greatest gift that he could ever have wished for in his wildest dreams; justice and freedom from the hellish nightmare that kept him chained for the last thirty years. He would no longer have to live in fear and pain; encased within the walls of loneliness and despair. With those few wonderful words, Stacey has set him free.

He turned to Eloise, who was holding her hands in front of her mouth, wide eyed and shaking from excitement, elation, relief, shame. James held out his hand and gently moved her arm so that she dropped her hands to her side and held them tightly. One moment she was smiling, laughing and then crying while tenderly kissing his hands. The woman on the chair remained seated but gaped at James in wonder. She was no longer capable of displaying her emotions; they had been frozen years ago.

After a few moments, when James managed to compose himself, he beckoned for Stacey to step closer to him. He grabbed her hands and enclosed them within both of his. 'Thank you,' he whispered, still choked up by the news. 'You must tell me everything.'

Stacey did just that to the last detail. The audience of three were mesmerised by all that she said. With every word, all the emotional torment that had wrapped itself around her, withered away until Stacey finally realised that she would be fine and could live a new life without Tom. It was not worth the effort of hanging onto something that in reality; never was.

She would still try to do whatever she could for Alice, Tom's mother. Now that Tom was gone from her life, did not mean that she would abandon the poor woman. Stacey would regularly visit her to make sure that she never felt alone. Michael, Tom's father was fine as long as he was kept in ignorance about what his son had done. Knowing the truth would only reopen old wounds and create further pain and suffering.

Ashley did mention that she had seen the priest that morning but Stacey quickly dismissed it from her mind. As far as she was concerned, Father Aiden was bound by the laws of the church and would never repeat a single word that was said during confession.

EPILOGUE

'For God's sake, will you just shut up!' Tom glared at Bradley who was sitting in the snow next to Ashley. He was on the verge of tears and was complaining that he was cold and hungry.

'Leave him alone, he's only five,' Ashley barked at Tom. She put her arm around her little brother to console him. Immediately, Bradley leaned closer to his sister but he kept his eyes firmly fixed on Tom.

'Yeah, too young to be out playing in the snow with us. Why in the hell did we have to take him with us? He'll ruin our day, just as he always does,' Tom growled sourly.

'Look, why don't you help me make this trench?' said Adam, trying to steer the attention away from Bradley, who was now quietly weeping. 'Ashley, why don't you and Bradley make some snowballs?'

Seeing that this was a good idea, Ashley stopped cuddling Bradley and gently helped him to stand up. 'Hey Brad, fancy making some snowballs with me so that we can throw them at each other?'

Bradley looked up at his sister, pouting. 'I don't want to, I'm freezing.'

'Stop moaning you little shit and do as your sister says,' Tom roared fiercely. 'Freak.'

Adam stopped digging deeper into the snow and stared at Tom, shocked that he could speak like that to his younger brother.

Ashley frowned. 'Tom, that's a horrible thing to say. What has got into you today?'

'Today was meant to be our day, away from that little twerp. It's not every day that it snows. He is getting on my nerves. One more time he moans and I don't know what I'll do.'

'Tom, just come over here and help me with the trench.' Adam pleaded. Tom's temperament was making him feel very uncomfortable.

Tom sighed and walked over to his friend and bent over to see how much he managed to dig. 'It's kind of neat I guess; you barely touched the ground beneath. God, the snow is so deep, it's brilliant.' He was clearly impressed. It was already about two feet deep. 'It's not a trench though, just a hole really.'

'You try digging snow with woolly gloves, my hands are numb now. I can't feel my fingers. Besides, the snow is quite hard. It must have frozen last night.' Adam smiled cheerfully.

'Don't be such a wimp.' Tom's humour appeared to have resurfaced. Adam had that effect on him. No matter how low he felt, Adam always managed to make him feel better.

'Look, I know Bradley gets on your nerves but your mum wanted us to take him out. Let Ashley look after him and we'll play soldiers. I found a couple of branches that will do for guns.' Adam bent down and picked up two thick pieces of wood that, with a little bit of imagination, were big enough to serve as machine guns.

Adam jumped into the hole and sufficiently crouched so that he could rest his gun on the snow above him. He pretended to look for any sign of the enemy and then loudly made the sound of a machine gun firing a shower of bullets. 'Ah-ah-ah-ah-ah.'

Tom watched for a moment and then turned his attention towards Ashley who was still trying to get Bradley to make snowballs. Tom could see that even she was getting in a bit of a fluster with Bradley. He was either folding his arms or slapping her on the arm. He could never understand where she got the patience from. He would have hit him by now.

Tom went over to them and said, 'Ashley, you stay with this thing.' He gave Bradley a quick kick on the leg. It was no more than a tap but Bradley screamed, grabbed Tom's leg and tried to bite it.

Tom shook him off and bellowed, 'Bloody animal.' He turned back to Adam, who had left the hole to stalk an invisible soldier. He stared at the place where the hole was and then turned back to Bradley, who again, burst out crying. 'You've done it now.' He bent down, grabbed Bradley and lifted him away from Ashley's side. He held him with extended arms in order to prevent being smacked by flaying arms and legs. Tom rapidly walked over to the hole. Bradley's face had turned red as he screamed with fear and kept on kicking and punching.

Tom flung Bradley into the hole, head first. There was a muffled thump and Bradley shrieked in pain.

Adam dropped his gun and ran back. He stopped a few feet from Tom. He didn't say anything but just watched, shocked by what he was seeing.

Ashley howled, 'Tom, stop hurting him. He's only little.'

Tom ignored both of them and stared down at the small boy who was clutching his head. Tears rolled down Bradley's face and he dribbled continuously as he cried out, 'Ashley.' His voice was thin and pitiful. Once more, he begged for his sister to help, 'Ashley, please.'

Tom jumped into the hole and grabbed hold of Bradley's hair and lifted him up. This made the boy scream even louder and he tried with all his might to kick, or punch his older brother. 'I'll make you shut up for good,' Tom snarled evilly. His nostrils flared and his eyes were like thunder.

Ashley whimpered at the sight and took a couple of steps back. Adam had grown incredibly pale and had begun to shake.

Tom lowered Bradley back into the hole and began relentlessly to punch and kick him. Every time his fist or boot connected with Bradley's body, there was a wet, meaty thud. Every blow was done with such force that the sound of snapping bones could be heard. As he continued with the brutality, he muttered breathlessly, 'You should never have been born, I hate you, you're just in the way all the time.'

At first, Bradley's shrieks were piercing and full of misery and pain. The sound tore through Ashley's and Adam's heads, as they watched with horror from a safe distance. What came next was even worse than Bradley's screams. The sudden silence was eerie and both of them knew that it was over; Bradley was dead.

Ashley began to sob while Adam fell down onto his knees and held his head in his hands. His face looked contorted with horror and grief.

Tom, for a fleeting moment, looked dazed as though he could not truly believe what he had done. He then panicked as he stared at his gloves and boots which were wet with blood. Hardly audible, he muttered, 'Got to hide this, got to do something to hide this.' Sharply, he surveyed the area and his eyes rested on something that was on the ground, a little to his left. On closer examination, Tom saw that it was a scarf. He turned back to where Bradley lay, inside the hole like a discarded rag doll. His arms were on either side of his head, reminding Tom of the times he had seen him sleeping snugly, safe in his bed.

After fetching the scarf with his blood sodden gloves, Tom strode purposefully towards the dead body and hollered at Ashley and Adam, 'Come on, help me.' He shoved Bradley's body with the tip of his foot until it was completely inside the hole. He dropped the scarf and then piled the snow on top of Bradley's corpse.

Ashley began to whimper when she could see that Tom was making a large snowman above her dead brother's shallow grave and burst into floods of tears when he picked up the scarf and wrapped it around the snowman's neck.

Adam stared at the gruesome sight and weakly whispered, 'What if he isn't dead? He'll suffocate under there.'

Ashley and Adam quickly glanced at each other but still did nothing. Their minds would always be troubled and their lives would never be the same. They were just as guilty of Bradley's death and that would haunt them forever.

Lightning Source UK Ltd.
Milton Keynes UK
UKOW04f1603030817
306612UK00001B/19/P